A SPARK IGNITES

www.MichaelLachmanWrites.com

SUDDEN IMPACT
PRESS

A Spark Ignites edited by Julie Hall
Walking the Wire edited by Chayala Nachum
A Sparked Interest edited by Zahava Lachman

Cover Art by Fabián Cobos
Cover Design by Michael Lachman

ISBN: 978-1-7365366-0-5

For my wife, Zahava.
This book wouldn't exist without you.

A SPARK IGNITES

MICHAEL LACHMAN

PROLOGUE

Night had long since fallen over the city. A lone figure stood atop the building, his silhouette outlined by the moon behind him. Clad in his black and blue high-tech super-suit, Spark peered down at the street below. His blond hair whipped in the chilled night air as his eyes narrowed, focusing on the pawn shop some sixty feet below. At this hour, even in the city that never sleeps, the shop was closed. The gaudy neon sign in the window was not aware of this fact, and flashed indiscriminately, advertising the small shop's wares. Over the past two weeks, three other pawn shops in the area had been burglarized. It was only a matter of time before this one was hit.

Spark tapped his foot impatiently. He'd already spent two fruitless nights staking out this location. He hoped tonight wouldn't be a third. Earlier that day, Spark overheard someone talking about how exciting the life of a superhero must be. Spark chuckled at the thought. The truth was, most of being a super hero was stakeouts and patrols. Heck, even half a dozen fights in a month was considered a lot.

It was in the silent moments like these that Spark wondered if he was making any difference. If he was gone, would crime actually rise in his absence? Was he wasting his time, running around in his pajamas stopping a petty thief here and there, while white-collar crime went unchecked? Did he even matter? Spark shook his head. He rarely came up with decent answers, and it did him no good to think about such things while on the job. A superhero who didn't have his head in the game would be a dead one before long.

The sound of faint rustling made Spark's hair stand on edge. He whirled around, looking for the source of the noise. The rooftop was empty. Spark, with gritted teeth, wondered if he'd just imagined it. He still couldn't shake the feeling like someone was watching him. These past couple of weeks, it felt as though someone was following him, stalking him— but no matter how hard he looked, he had yet to find any evidence to support that conclusion. Still, the shadows and flashes in the corner of his vision couldn't just be his imagination, right? Spark shook his head. He was being paranoid again.

Even against the noise of the city, the abrupt sound of glass shattering broke through the cacophony that made up the city's soundtrack. Spark looked down at the thrift shop's broken window, turning his thoughts from paranoia and other heavy contemplations to the simple job at hand. He jumped off the building and smiled as the ground rushed up at him. The thief cried out as he spotted the hero approaching. Spark smiled. This was simple. This, he *knew*.

There was work to be done.

CHAPTER ONE

Matt Stone panted as his feet rhythmically slammed the pavement. He stopped to catch his breath, and continued on his way. Winded, he walked at a brisk pace rather than run, cursing silently. Matt was late to school again, for the second time that month. His stupid brother Evan woke him up at three in the morning yet again, and it had taken him a while to fall back asleep.

As if being in college gives Evan the right, Matt fumed, keeping a tight pace, his hands clenched into fists. Evan's still living at home. He shouldn't be allowed to come and go at all hours of the night. The house isn't a Seven-Eleven.

Matt ran his hands through his blond hair. It was wet with perspiration. *Wonderful*, he thought. *Now I'll smell like sweat the whole day.* The school was coming up, just across the street. It was an old, dirty, unremarkable red-bricked building with faded, withered vines that had snaked across the left wall so long ago, it seemed like it was part of it. Matt figured the building probably hadn't changed much since the time his father had attended school there. His blood boiled, thinking of Evan as he crossed the street. A car honked as it drove past him; his hazel eyes flashed as he yelled at the driver, who was too far away at this point for the sound waves to reach his ears. Matt cursed again under his breath. He hated the whole concept of cities. He despised the noise and detested the concrete canyons the buildings formed. *This many people weren't meant to live this close together.*

Matt sighed. He wished he lived in a place filled with sprawling lawns and rows of trees. He'd trade grey for green any day.

Matt's sour mood continued as he walked into class. He didn't like being late. Especially *this* late, when it meant he'd missed history class entirely. He actually *liked* history. As Matt reached the room for his second period math class, he took a deep breath. *Here we go.*

Ms. Wilson, who was in the middle of writing a math equation on the board, stopped as Matt walked in. She was an old, frail-looking woman with hanging jowls that made her appear even older than she was. Her white hair was always in a bun with at least two pencils stuck in it, and she was rarely seen without her rainbow shawl, even in hot weather. As she turned toward Matt, her loose jowls shook.

"Mr. Stone. You're late," she said, stating the obvious. The woman sounded tired. Stopping the class to berate one late child was not something she took pleasure in anymore.

"Yeah, sorry. I overslept," He replied sheepishly. He heard a few kids laughing. "It won't happen again."

Ms. Wilson sighed. "See that it doesn't." She motioned to Matt's desk. "Please take your seat."

Matt took his familiar seat behind Amy Hunter as Miss Wilson turned back to the board. Amy turned her head towards Matt, her brown eyes sparkling.

"You've never been *this* late before. What happened?" she whispered. She didn't really have to whisper; Ms. Wilson didn't have the greatest of hearing.

"Evan," he replied simply.

Amy chuckled as she redid her ponytail, her hands clasping her brown hair. "I'm so glad I only have a *little* brother."

"Yeah, Evan can be a real jerk sometimes. I wish I was an only child."

Matt glanced at Ms. Wilson, who was drawing a graph. The chalk in her hand broke in two. She mumbled something as she furiously grabbed the box on her desk for another piece. This was probably the only school in the state that still used an old fashioned chalkboard, by Matt's estimate.

"You don't really think that," Amy whispered, her ponytail settling behind her.

Matt shrugged.

There was a snapping sound, drawing Matt and Amy's attention to the front of the room. One of their classmates was in front of the board, trying to solve the equation. Miss Wilson was snapping her fingers at the two, and putting her other finger to her mouth, indicating they be quiet. Matt slumped back into his seat and put his head down.

"Hey," he heard Amy whisper. "Do you smell like sweat?"

"Amy," he said dryly, lifting his head. "Shut up."

Matt's mood didn't improve all that much by the time he reached his house.

"I'm home," he yelled out to no one in particular.

There was no response. Matt wasn't surprised; his parents were rarely home before eight. He tramped upstairs to his room, pulled out his key, and unlocked the door. Matt had fought his parents for several months to get that lock on his door. Like all seventeen-year-olds, his privacy was very important to him.

The room wasn't big by any standards, but that was all part of living in Brooklyn. He didn't mind that though. The room was a drab, pale color Matt couldn't quite describe. His parents had repeatedly promised to repaint the walls, but despite Matt's badgering, they never did. He had a bed to sleep in, a dresser and closet for his clothes, a bookshelf that housed his favorite novels, and a desk on which his computer rested; he didn't need more than that. Matt grabbed a book from the bookshelf, a murder mystery he was in the midst of reading, and reached for his iPad that he'd left lying on his desk the other day. His hand hit the hard wood with a dull thud. Matt looked down. Nothing. His iPad was gone. Did he put it somewhere else and forgot? No, he was sure he'd left it on the desk. And the door was locked. The blood rushed to his face as the realization set in. *Evan.*

Matt remembered Evan used to be passionate about magic when he was younger, and although he eventually replaced that obsession with superheroes, Evan never forgot how to pick locks. And boy was it frickin' annoying. Matt cursed and threw the book on his bed and stomped out of his room, toward Evan's room across the hall.

As Matt barged into Evan's room, he was greeted by a bunch of superhero posters, both fictional and real, which were adorning the walls and covering nearly every flat surface. Matt rolled his eyes. He looked around the room, which was slightly larger than his, hoping to find his stolen device. Evan was out, most likely in college. Matt just didn't have the energy to deal with him at the moment. Then he spotted it. There, openly lying on the bed, was Matt's iPad. Matt grabbed it and stormed back to his room, slamming the door behind him.

"Jerk," he muttered under this breath.

CHAPTER TWO

The man pushed a cardboard box of wires against the wall. He felt undignified. Here he was, in his signature white lab coat, moving boxes like a common henchman. He kicked himself for not building a robot maid, like on that old Hanna-Barbera cartoon, The Jetsons. As he stacked one box atop another, a tower of boxes next to him fell over. He grunted in frustration.

Alan Swift was annoyed. He had spent the better part of an hour trying to make the room presentable enough for his client, but the room was still a mess. A chalkboard covered in complicated equations was leaning lopsided against a wall, which was lined with television screens. In the middle of the room stood two chairs beside a large table that looked hastily cleared off, save for a few nuts and bolts, a wire, and a pile of various laptops. Half of the floor was clean, making a clear path from the door to the table, while the other half was piled high with pieces of metal and circuit boards. This wasn't just Alan's meeting room. It was where he worked, and it showed. He pushed a half-built robot out of the way. He'd finish that later. The room had to look semi-presentable, at least.

Alan paced the floor. He didn't like doing this, but hey, it paid the bills. Most people in Alan's position would've founded a big internet startup, or invent the next smartphone. But all that was too boring for Alan. No, being a genius with a 162 IQ meant he didn't have to take the expected path through life. He fancied himself an artist of sorts. But his performance art, like everything, costs money. Jetpacks and robot armies don't grow on trees, after all. And to get money, sometimes Alan would have to take jobs he'd rather not, such as consulting or inventing for others. Especially now, when he had a brilliant scheme for what could be his best performance yet. It was still a good six months away and required a huge budget—which was why Alan had begun taking on three times his usual level of clients.

Alan looked out the window and noticed his reflection. When did he get so old? His hair had begun to gray, and he noticed some lines that he was sure weren't there the day before. The doorbell rang. Alan sighed. So his client had actually arrived. Alan pressed a button on his watch. There was a buzz as the door behind him opened. Alan turned around to greet the man.

Standing in the doorway was his client, shifting awkwardly as he gazed at the mess inside. If he was trying to hide his discomfort being there, he didn't do a very good job. The man wore an expensive Italian suit, and had his blond hair slicked back with some sort of gel. Alan found himself admiring the client's Adonis-like features. Sure, he'd seen him on television and the internet, but it was something else, seeing him in person. The man's square jaw and magnificently sharp cheekbones looked almost unreal, more like a computer-generated rendering of a person rather than actual flesh and blood. His bright green eyes narrowed as he looked at Alan.

Alan greeted the man. "Come in, Mr.—"

"Don't use my name," he said quickly. Alan noticed the man had a device clipped to the collar of his shirt emitting a bright light. Of course. It was an infrared LED, which stops video devices from recording the area around it, namely the client's face.

This man is awfully paranoid, Alan thought. "Of course, whatever you say, *sir*," Alan said, showing the client to a seat.

The man's eyes fell on the table. A look of disdain crawled across his face as he carefully sat down on the chair beside it. The client began speaking. "So, Mr. Swift? Or is it Dr. Swift?"

"Actually, I prefer the pseudonym 'the Inventor.'"

The client chuckled. "The Inventor? You still fancy yourself a supervillain?"

"I fancy myself an inventor," Alan replied, matter-of-factly. *Although yes, I do consider myself a supervillain,* he thought silently. *One of the best.*

The client nodded as he straightened his cuff link. "Yes, well it's that talent of yours that I require. So that thing we discussed on the phone earlier, is it possible?"

"Well, it'll certainly be a challenge. I assume it is for military application?"

"You could say that, yes. It will be used to fight a war, certainly." He smiled as though he had just told a private joke. "But what it's used for isn't your concern."

"No, I suppose it isn't." Alan's eyes narrowed. He didn't trust the man. But a client was a client, and this one certainly had the resources to pay, and pay well.

"It *can* be done though, right? You *can* build it, can't you, Inventor?" the client asked intently. The man seemed almost desperate.

"A device that can destroy something by honing in on its vibrational frequency?" Alan chuckled. "Nicola Tesla was capable of locating specific frequencies. And not merely radio waves, either. According to some accounts, apocryphal or not, he had determined the frequencies of buildings, earth, and stone, and with such knowledge was capable of destroying said buildings by matching the frequencies. Not to say he would have done such a thing, his moral compass was far stronger than mine. And whether this was true or not is not of any consequence. The important thing is that the science holds up, it is possible, and I'm going to do it. I'm sure I can."

The Inventor glanced at his client, hoping for his approval. The man smiled, but it was eerie. Snakelike. A soulless smile. A chill went up the Inventor's spine. He hated clients.

CHAPTER THREE

Matt walked into school, late yet again for the second time this week. At least he was only a few minutes late, which meant he didn't miss history class. Matt raced down the hall. When he got to the room, he burst in, making a louder noise than he intended. Mr. Winter leered at Matt as he sheepishly walked toward his seat. The man had a ruddy complexion and a full face. His white hair had recently begun noticeably thinning.

Matt walked to the middle of the room and sat down at his desk. Dan, sitting in the row across, looked at Matt quizzically, as if to ask why he was late. Matt just gave him one look that explained everything.

Evan. Again.

Dan smirked and nodded.

Matt noted Dan wasn't wearing his glasses today, a rarity for him. He must be trying out a new pair of contact lenses. Matt doubted it would last.

Dan Raye had been Matt's best friend since second grade, and although he often started things enthusiastically, he didn't usually see them through. This would be his third attempt to stop wearing his glasses. Or fourth. Matt couldn't remember.

Mr. Winter continued on with his lesson. "As I was saying, it's Tuesday, so we're once again going to discuss current events and the history that led to those events. Any suggestions?"

A redheaded girl raised her hand. Mr. Winter motioned at her with his hand. "Yes, Jaimie?"

Matt found it strange how he always referred to girls by their first name but boys by their last. Amy had told Matt it made some of the girls in the class feel uneasy.

"Dragonfly was on the news last night," Jaimie said. "He caught a few people breaking into a bank or something."

"It was an electronics store," Dan called out. His hands immediately slapped his forehead, pushing his messy brown hair from his face.

Matt chuckled as Dan lowered his eyes. One doesn't just call out in Mr. Winter's class.

Mr. Winter mouth stretched into a shark-like grin. "Mr. Raye, thank you for sharing that with us. Now, if you're such an expert in the matter, can you tell the class who said, 'You can't let yourself be pushed around. You can't live in fear. That's no way to live your life.'?"

Dan paused for a moment, as if unsure. "Wasn't that Bernie Goetz, the Subway Vigilante?"

Matt smiled. Dan often geeked out about things like Doctor Who or Pokémon, becoming obsessed until he gained an encyclopedic knowledge of said subject before promptly losing interest. But the only thing that Dan's been obsessed with forever, without losing any interest, was superheroes. When it came to that subject, he was usually the most knowledgeable person in the room. The only other person who Matt knew was as obsessed with superheroes as Dan was Evan.

Mr. Winter blinked, surprised. "Er, yes, it was. The superhero phenomenon, although yes, based somewhat on comic books, had no real life counterpart until Bernard Goetz took the law into his own hands on December 22, 1984, right here in New York. That sparked a whole wave of vigilantes, mostly costumed, throughout the country. Now, you kids don't remember this, but there used to be nearly a dozen of them for every major city, as opposed to the two or three we have now."

Matt raised his hand. "Mr. Stone," the teacher said, pointing to him. "Speak."

"Why do the police continue to look the other way? Isn't vigilantism illegal?"

"That's a good question," Mr. Winter said as he began pacing. "Can anyone answer? Mr. Barnes?" He pointed to a tall olive skinned boy in the front of the classroom.

"Because they help out, and don't, like, kill people?"

"Yes, as soon as someone dies, kills someone, their identity is discovered, or they fall out of public favor, it usually isn't long before they're arrested. You all remember Captain Impossible?" Everyone other than Dan stared at Mr. Winter with blank faces. "Oh, c'mon? Captain Impossible? He was—" He trailed off and sighed. "I'm old," he mumbled.

Matt raised his hand again, and Mr. Winter nodded. "My brother owns over half a dozen autobiographies of superheroes. How does that happen?"

"Some heroes, and some so called supervillains too, for that matter, write books or sell the movie rights after they win their court case, after the statute of limitations runs out, or after their time in prison. You guys saw the Doctor Shadow TV movie last year, right?"

Again, other than Dan, a class full of blank stares.

"No?" He sighed again.

Matt stifled a laugh.

"Okay class, well that's enough. I feel like an old-timer. Now open up your books. If you remember, we left off last class with the tension between the northern and southern states reaching critical levels."

Matt smiled. There was something about history that he loved. The idea of passing down knowledge, a legacy, from one generation to the next. It created a form of continuity in life. He felt the past directly influenced the future, and gave meaning to life, which would, after a time, itself become history. Matt opened his textbook excitedly.

The cafeteria was crowded, as usual. Matt sat down next to Dan and Amy. His lunch tray clattered as he dropped it down on the table. The tray was filled with some sort of green and brown stew-like substance, and some nuggets, though Matt couldn't tell if it was supposed to be chicken or something else. He looked at Amy across the table, eating her homemade chicken salad. She always made herself lunch in the morning to bring to school. Matt didn't wake up nearly early enough for that, though he wondered at the moment if his sleep was really worth it.

Amy noticed Matt looking at her food and moved her container slightly away from him, causing him to look up at her. She smirked playfully and winked. Dan was oblivious to all this dutifully devouring his school lunch, as though he'd been fasting all day. Matt pushed away his tray.

"Are you finished eating?" Dan asked.

Matt looked at Dan strangely. It wasn't usual for Dan to eat so much. Had he missed breakfast or something?

"It's yours," Matt said.

"So, about what we were discussing in class earlier today," Dan said with a mouthful of food.

Matt interrupted Dan. "Man, chew with your mouth closed. We're in the presence of a lady!"

Matt gestured at Amy. She gave him a disapproving look as she folded her arms. Matt had known Amy practically all his life. They even had sleepovers as little kids. He knew she didn't like being called a lady. Although implying she wasn't one was probably worse.

"Oh, Amy's no lady!" Dan said, chuckling. Amy shot him a look. Dan swallowed his food with a big gulp as his face turned red. "Sorry, I was kidding." Matt laughed.

Amy smiled. "So what'd you guys discuss in class today?"

"Superheroes," Matt said before Dan could answer. "Dan's favorite topic."

Amy giggled.

"Hey, they totally save people!" Dan said a little louder than was necessary, as though he'd just been insulted. "And remember, they're real people like you and me. They're not comic book characters. They don't have powers."

"But what do they do, really?" Matt asked. "I mean, they fight bad guys, sure, but most of them are just out for the glory. Half these guys just want to be famous. They don't really care about other people."

"You don't know that," Dan said defensively. "Besides, there are worse ways to get famous, like being a reality star or something."

"Is it? There've been studies that indicate that supervillains only appeared to counter the masked vigilantes, like a form of escalation."

"That theory has never been proven."

They both looked at Amy, as though she were a judge.

"Hey, don't look at me. I know enough to know I'm not well-versed enough in the subject to have an informed opinion. Now how about we have a conversation involving something we can all talk about."

"Like some girly movie or something?" Matt said smile.

Dan laughed. "Yeah, like The Notebook?"

"Oh, I've never actually seen that," Amy said. The two looked at her with jaws slacked, a look of shock across their faces.

"You've never seen The Notebook?" Dan exclaimed.

"Wow," Matt said. "You've got to be like, the only girl I've ever met who hasn't seen it."

Amy shrugged. "Maybe I haven't seen it because I'm not a lady," she said looking at Dan.

His ears turned red as he smiled sheepishly. The bell rang, indicating the end of lunch period. The three got up to go to their respective classes. Matt's stomach growled. He wished he'd eaten that lunch.

CHAPTER FOUR

The vibrational frequency device was proceeding as scheduled and the money he was receiving from the most recent client should tide him over for at least the next few months. That wasn't why Alan was excited though. It was finally time for another one of his performances. Well, another one of *the Inventor's* performances.

Alan was standing atop a building, where he was sure he'd be seen by his target. He was wearing his trademark white lab coat, and was making some last-minute adjustments to the robot. Due to the bright lights of the city, the robot was clearly visible, despite it being night. The lights reflected off its metallic skeletal casing. It had an oval head with two huge eyes and no mouth. The eyes were just for show, of course. Heck, most of the head was pointless. Alan had actually put all the relevant censors and cameras in its chest. He was particularly proud of this model, and couldn't wait to test it.

He wasn't going to rob any place. He rarely did. Successfully, anyway. Sure, if he really wanted to, he could succeed. Heck, he could probably kill nearly every hero in the tri-state area if he cared to. But that wasn't the point. The point of these little adventures was to test the hero, not money, not fame, and not power. Playing the game was its own reward. Alan didn't mind that his 'failures' made him a 'b-list' villain. He did it for the love of the craft. He did it for the art.

One had to wonder why it was that he'd been at it for a decade, while he'd seen dozens of heroes come and go. Villains seemed to have much more longevity than the heroes. Sure, occasionally one would get killed, but ninety percent of the time, the villain would, at worst, get caught and sent to prison, where he or she would be out before long and back to his or her old tricks. Alan smiled. He'd never been caught.

Alan had a theory about why the villains lasted longer than the heroes, of course. He had a theory for just about everything. The heroes were out every night, risking their lives, while the villains were only out one night a week at best. It wasn't just chance though. It was the rules. The heroes always play by the rules. They won't kill, and it was oh so easy to use that against them. Most villains, however, don't play by the rules, which puts them at a distinct advantage. But the Inventor *did* play by the rules. Alan wore that as a badge of pride. Ten years of being a supervillain, one major performance every month, and not a single casualty. That was something to be proud of.

He looked at his watch. If Spark kept to his patrol schedule, he would be there soon. Alan put on his jetpack and patted the robot on the head.

"Don't let me down, boy."

Alan pressed a button on his watch. There was a faint whirring sound as the robot stood up straight. Its eyes began to glow green, and its hands folded into fists. Alan slipped away into the shadows, but still within eyesight. It wouldn't be long now.

After waiting a few minutes, there was a flash of black and blue as Spark landed on the building. He stood up, his blond hair rippling in the breeze. The mask covered his face from the forehead down, and the suit was black, with a few lines of blue, and of course the iconic blue Spark logo. Alan watched from the shadows. He had always admired the suit. It was certainly high-tech, with strength enhancement and flight capability, and of course, the electronically-charged gloves that was—he assumed—where Spark took his name from. Alan figured he could probably build a suit like that for himself, but he always found the 'evil clone' approach to villainy to be cheap and uninspired. He was better than that.

Spark tilted his head as he looked at the robot. "What the heck is that?" Spark said to no one in particular.

The robot jerked its head, turning it to face Spark. A voice emanated from it. "Spark! Prepare to die!" it said in Alan's voice.

Alan didn't want to spend money hiring a voice actor, and it was either that or use the monotone Stephen Hawking voice that he'd downloaded online. Vanity made him choose the former.

Without a word, Spark stepped back alarmed, and shifted into a fighting stance. Spark didn't talk or throw around quips all that much, something Alan wished he could change. It detracted from the performance.

The robot lifted its hands in Spark's direction, while the hands shifted and transformed into chainsaws. Alan watched gleefully. Oh, he didn't actually expect Spark to die. Heck, Spark would probably win. When one plays by the rules like Alan, the hero usually does. The question was, how long it would take Spark to figure out how to disable it?

The robot suddenly raced toward Spark, moving much faster than it looked like it was capable of, its chainsaw hands swinging wildly. Spark dove out of the way, the blades missing him by a hairsbreadth.

Alan marveled at the choreography. It was beautiful and graceful. He patted himself on the back.

Spark landed next to a bat that Alan had carefully placed in that area earlier, lifting it up to defend himself. He was knocked to the floor, the robot already on top of him, sparks flying as it tried to cut through the bat. Spark pushed the pole at an angle, shifting the robot's weight. The robot's arms crossed as it tried to right itself. There was a loud clang as one of its chainsaw arms fell to the floor, its whirring slowly fading.

Alan winced. Even knowing how things would likely play out, it still stung a bit every time he saw something he built break.

With one arm missing, it took a moment for the robot to adjust its balance. Spark used the opportunity to press the button on his glove, causing electricity to dance around the palm of his hand. He touched the robot's chest, but it had no effect. Alan smiled as he watched. Spark had acted exactly as he expected.

The robot knocked Spark with its broken arm, the sharp pieces cutting his shoulder. Spark yelped in pain, and backed up, eyes searching for a weakness. Blood dripped down his arm. He swung the baseball bat at the robot's head, knocking it clean off.

Alan grabbed his mouth to stop himself from laughing. He couldn't wait to see how Spark would react when he'd realize removing the head would have no effect at all.

"You'll have to try harder than that!" the robot said in Alan's voice, as it continued to walk toward Spark, swinging its good arm.

"Catch me!" Spark yelled as he ran toward the rooftop water tank.

The headless robot pursued, slashing at Spark. Alan reveled in the battle. This was the climax he'd been building toward. As the chainsaw cut through the wall of the tank, water rushed out, hitting the robot. There was a piercing noise as the robot, now soaked, slowed down to an eventual stop.

"Inventor!" Spark yelled. "I know you're here!"

Alan took a deep breath. This was his cue. He jumped into the air, his jetpack on, allowing him to fly high above Spark. In his left hand was a clothed dummy. From far enough away, it would look like a person. At least that's what he hoped. Alan still wasn't sure just how good

Spark's night vision was, or if he had a magnifying lens. But hey, the risks were all part of the fun.

Alan yelled the lines he'd previously rehearsed into the small microphone clipped onto his lapel. "Curses! Spark, you've defeated my robot! You'll pay for that!"

Some people accused Alan of being cheesy, blaming him for the reason people didn't take supervillains seriously. Alan liked to think of his performances as classic.

"Not that it matters," he continued, his voice reaching Spark through a carefully hidden speaker. "This was just a minor part of my plan, easily remedied. You haven't seen the last of me!"

It was all a lie, of course, but he was sure it'd keep Spark paranoid for a few weeks at least.

Spark jumped into the air after him. Alan wasn't worried. His jetpack was faster than Spark's rocket boots anyway. But to cover his bases, Alan dropped the dummy.

"No!" Spark yelled as he dove to catch the dummy.

Alan laughed. By the time Spark discovered the dummy wasn't a person, Alan would be safely out of sight. As performances go, it wasn't his best. But Alan viewed it more as a rehearsal anyway, and was proud of it nonetheless.

CHAPTER FIVE

Robert and Marilyn Stone were workaholics. As such, it was rare that Matt ever saw his parents during the week. They left to work early in the morning and arrived home fairly late, usually going to bed within an hour after arriving. Matt didn't mind it so much, especially due to the freedom it allowed, but at times he thought it would've been nice to have someone pack him lunch, make him dinner, or even just ask him about his day. So this morning, Matt was surprised to find his mother still home.

As he walked downstairs, already dressed, with his knapsack over his shoulder, he heard his mother's voice coming from the kitchen. He raced in to find her talking on the phone. Marilyn had a narrow face that was always caked in makeup, and the kind of body that even while sitting down, you could tell she was tall. Matt often wondered where her height went, as neither he nor Evan were particularly tall. If not for her blonde hair, Matt would've thought he and Evan were adopted. She sat at the table with a steaming cup of coffee, talking animatedly on the phone. She looked up as Matt walked in, and held up a finger.

"Yeah, so I have to go. I'll call you back. Okay, okay, bye." She hung up the phone and turned her attention back to Matt. "What's up, kiddo?"

"What are you doing home?"

Marilyn laughed. "Oh, yes, well I quit my job. I guess I forgot to tell you."

"Whoa," Matt said excitedly. Now he'd actually have a mother. "That's great! Good for you!"

"Thanks, sweetie," she said with a smile. "But it's only for today. I start at a new firm tomorrow."

"Oh." Matt couldn't help but feel disappointed.

"Yeah, we'll finally have more money coming in! Isn't that great?" Marilyn seemed very excited.

"Yeah, Mom. Great," Matt replied, trying to hide his dissatisfaction. He reminded himself that absent parents are better than fighting parents. At least he didn't have to go through what Dan had to go through every day.

She gave him a sideways look. "Aren't you late for school?"

Matt glanced up at the clock and cursed silently. He grabbed a granola bar from the pantry and stuffed it into his pocket.

"See you, Mom!" he said as he ran out. "Though I doubt it'll be anytime soon," he added as soon as he was out of earshot.

Amy Hunter ran into Jaimie on the way to school.

"Hey, how're you doing?" Jaimie asked.

"Fine, you?" Amy answered, knowing good and well that when someone asks that, they're really just saying 'hello.' No one actually wants an honest answer about how you're doing, especially not in high school.

"Good, you?" Jaime responded.

Amy wasn't sure how to reply. The way the conversation was going they could be stuck in some kind of time loop. She giggled at her own internal commentary.

Jaimie must've realized what she just said because she laughed awkwardly. "Sorry about that. Hey, I was wondering, are you and Stone an item?"

Amy laughed. "Matt? No, we're just friends. Really good friends though. Why?"

Jaimie began running her hands through her crimson hair. "No reason. I mean, he's cute, isn't he? If he wasn't so short, I mean."

"Yeah, I guess. But so what? We're just friends. Totally platonic. And yeah, he is kind of short." Amy laughed.

Jaimie rolled her eyes. "Hunter, there's no such thing as guys and girls who are just platonic friends. It doesn't exist."

"Well, I don't think of him that way. Or Dan, for that matter."

"Okay, Dan's a dork, he doesn't count."

Amy made a face. She knew she should say something to defend Dan's honor, but remained silent. She felt guilty.

"And if you don't think of Matt in that way, let me tell you, he thinks of you that way. Heck, Dan does too, I'll bet."

Amy rolled her eyes. "And what makes you so sure?"

"I'm like, a relationship expert," Jaimie said confidently as the two walked through the school gates. "I've been in over *fifteen* relationships, so I know how this stuff works."

Amy stifled a laugh. Jaimie was only seventeen, like her. If Jaimie had been in over fifteen relationships at this point in her young life, all that meant was she knew how *bad* relationships work.

"I'll take your advice under consideration," Amy finally replied wryly.

She noticed a splash of yellow in the corner of her eyes. Across the pavement was Dan's sneakers, each pair lying on the ground near the school's brick wall, several feet from each other. Despite always dressing neatly and professionally, with a tucked-in button-down shirt and a pressed pair of pants or jet black jeans, Dan was rarely seen without his pair of neon yellow sneakers. At the moment, he was not far away from his precious sneakers, as he stumbled in his white socks toward them, face red.

Jaimie laughed, her red curls bobbing. Amy ignored her as she ran toward Dan, who at this point had grabbed one of his sneakers and shoved it onto his feet. He began tying it angrily. When Dan looked up, Amy was there holding out his other sneaker, a look of concern on her face.

"Thanks," Dan grumbled as he grabbed the sneaker from her and began putting it on.

"Are you okay? Do you want to talk about it?" she asked.

Dan scowled as he looked at his laces intently and tied them. When he looked up at Amy, his expression softened.

"Sorry. No, I just— I mean—" He sighed. "How long will I have to deal with this? Things at home are awful, you know?"

"Right, with your parents," Amy said. Dan's parents fought a lot. There was a reason she and Matt never went over to his place.

"Yeah, and school and my internship are supposed to be my escape, and work is fine, but this place?" Dan exhaled. "Sometimes I think I'd rather be home. Steve's really starting to get to me."

Amy nodded. Dan was talking about Steve Sakurai, a beefy kid in their grade who'd made bullying Dan his new hobby this year. Amy figured he's the one who wrestled away Dan's sneakers and threw them. She knew she couldn't interfere. Not really. In high school, everyone had to deal with their own problems. If Amy stepped in, she'd probably make things worse.

"I don't know what to tell you, Dan. But it does get easier."

"How would *you* know?"

"Things can't really get much worse, so they have to get better."

Dan leered at her. "Things are never so bad that they can't get worse. They can *always* get worse."

Amy sighed. "You're right. But, well, you'll eventually be out of high school, and you can dorm at college. You can start over there."

"That's over a year away," Dan grumbled.

"I know. And it seems like forever. But it'll be here soon enough."

Dan grunted.

Amy rolled her eyes. "What, you think you're the first person Steve's picked on?" she said angrily. "Matt and I went to middle school with the jerk. He used to throw pennies at Matt all the time!"

Dan looked puzzled. "Pennies?" Then he nodded as the realization hit him. "Oh, because he's Jewish."

"Yeah. And Matt took it. Just ignored him. Eventually, after a year or so, he moved on to someone else."

Dan clenched his hands into fists. "So what you're saying is I should continue to take it for over a year, and *maybe* he'll get bored?"

"No, what you *should* do is stand up to him, but we both know you won't. My point is, everyone had garbage to deal with at one point or another. Everyone. That doesn't make what you have less important, it just—" Amy took a deep breath. She closed her eyes and exhaled before opening them. "Okay, that was not going *at all* where I planned it. Just know that you have friends. Matt and I are here for you. You don't have to go through this alone."

Dan stared at her, shocked for a moment, then grabbed her into a hug. Amy's eyes opened wide, then a faint smile crossed her lips.

Matt appeared out of nowhere, leaning over and panting, holding his chest as he tried to catch his breath.

"I'm not late," he said with a strained voice. "How about that?" He looked up, to see Dan and Amy hugging. "Whoa! What'd I miss?"

Dan released Amy and smiled awkwardly. "Oh, nothing," he said.

Matt looked at Amy with a raised eyebrow, as if expecting her to answer. Amy just shrugged. "Were you guys talking about Rose?" Matt asked.

He was referring to Rose Ryan, Dan's longtime crush. Even after being interested in her for years, Dan still had yet to actually speak to her. Amy looked at Dan, who was expressionless, and shrugged again. The bell rang and the three walked to class.

CHAPTER SIX

To others, the room must've looked messy, but to Alan Swift, everything was in its place. He had two laptops open, one playing footage of Spark on a loop, with the other displaying lines upon lines of code. Alan enjoyed watching footage of his previous performances, and always made sure to have a camera or two set up to record it. The table he sat at was full of wires, transducers, transistors, and numerous other various electronic components. This was Alan's place. Doing this, surrounded by this—that was what made him happy.

The phone rang. Alan sighed in frustration. He hated talking to people on the phone. Why couldn't his clients just text, like normal people? *Because they're old*, he told himself. *Just like you.* He picked up the phone. "What?"

"Inventor? I'm paying you, quite well, I might add. The least you could do is talk to me with the proper respect," said the client in an angry tone.

"Fine. What, *please*?"

The line was silent for a moment, as though the client was considering whether this blatant lack of respect was worth wasting any more time on. Finally, the client spoke up. "The vibrational frequency device, is it finished?"

"Yeah, just about. I'm just making some finishing touches on the prototype. I'll email you the plans later today along with the necessary software code, so you can produce it yourself in whatever quantities you want."

"Don't email it. Just overnight the plans and send the software code on a flash drive. I don't want a digital trail."

Alan rolled his eyes. This had to be his most paranoid client yet.

The man continued. "And you're sure it works?"

"No," Alan said honestly. "It *should*, but I'm not sure. I'll be testing the prototype out tomorrow. You'll have the plans in your hands by then. Just don't put anything into production until you hear if it works."

"Sounds reasonable. You'll call me with the results tomorrow, I assume."

Alan grinned. "I shouldn't have to. Just watch the news."

"Now hold on a sec—"

Alan hung up. He was actually excited about testing the device out. Tomorrow could be his best performance in years, and his second performance within one week. He'd never done that before.

And there'll be an audience this time, he thought excitedly.

The plan was simple. He'd rob a bank, using the vibrational frequency device to destroy the vault by setting it to the frequency of reinforced steel. He glanced at the device lying on the table. It looked like a toy gun, made with cheap-looking white plastic, wires sticking out of one of the opened sections, and a small antenna surrounded by a little protective dish at the end. It was still unfinished and larger than he'd have liked. He could've made it smaller, but he was on a deadline. No doubt the client would be able to shrink it, considering his resources.

Alan looked at the clock. So much work to do and so little time. He sighed, grabbed a circuit board and his protective goggles. It was time to get to work.

The man stood motionless, staring at the phone in his palm. He was still trying to process that someone had hung up on him. No *one* hangs up on him. He angrily threw the phone on the floor, where it clattered loudly.

He looked around the room. The walls were bare, just the way he liked it, and painted a light teal. He didn't have an opinion on the color, but just the same, the man figured it might be time to repaint the room. There were three other men in the room with him. Two of his security guards, and an engineer.

The client turned to the engineer, who looked as though he was young enough to still be in college, and sported a trimmed beard.

"The blueprints will be here tomorrow. You will find a way to implement the device into the current design of the product. No one else will know of this," the client said with authority.

"Sure," said the engineer. "I'll try."

"You *will*."

"I will, yeah. But, do you mind telling me what it's for?" the engineer asked. "I need to know."

"No, you really don't," the client said coldly.

He sighed. He hated getting things dirty. The client swiftly reached into his jacket pocket, whipped out a gun, and shot the engineer in the leg. The deafening sound of the gunshot echoed through the empty room. The man dropped to the floor, screaming in pain. Blood had sprayed all over. As he held his leg, red fluid covered his fingers. The engineer's eyes began to water.

The client remained emotionless. "So we're agreed?" he asked calmly.

The engineer nodded, clutching his leg. "Whatever you say, sir."

"Much better." The client smiled. "Thank you. I'll sleep better at night." He turned toward one of his security guards. "You, see that the boy is patched up. I'll compensate him for his injuries accordingly."

The guard grunted and nodded. As the client left the room with the bleeding man, the other security guard followed him out. The client paused and turned his head back, surveying the room again.

"Oh, and someone see that the room is repainted. The blood splatter looks garish."

CHAPTER SEVEN

Matt walked through the door. Home at last. He noticed his mother's car was missing from the driveway, which meant she wasn't home. No surprise there. He threw down his backpack and walked down the hall toward the kitchen.

I really ought to stop skipping lunch, he thought.

It had been lasagna today, at least that's what they had claimed. Matt was pretty sure it was some form of edible plastic.

He opened the fridge and scanned the contents. Nothing. Nothing worth eating, anyway. Then again, Matt was a picky eater. As he closed the fridge, his stomach growled in protest. Matt lowered his standards and opened the fridge again. After rummaging through the contents long enough for the motor to start up, Matt finally picked up an apple, taking a chunk out of it as he slammed the door shut. It was surprisingly sweet. He'd have to remember to put yellow apples on the list of foods he'll actually eat. Suddenly the apple was gone, yanked from his hands.

"Thanks, Matty," Evan said with a smile as he chewed a bite from the apple resting in his hands.

Evan Stone looked very similar to Matt, and it was never a surprise when anyone found out they were brothers. Like Matt, he had blond hair and hazel eyes, and a thin face. Evan was bigger though, both in height and muscle, and had more pronounced cheekbones.

Matt glowered. "C'mon man, I was eating that!"

Evan laughed. "I said 'thank you.' What do you want, a parade?"

Matt crossed his arms, glaring.

Evan rolled his eyes as he took another apple out of the fridge and threw it at Matt. "Happy now?"

Matt wordlessly took a bite out of the apple as he walked out of the room. He really hated Evan sometimes.

"So Matty," Evan said, following behind him. "Any chance Dan's coming over?" For whatever reason, Evan and Dan were actually friends. Matt couldn't figure it out.

"No, he got an internship now at FalconTech. He goes there every day after school."

"Oh," Evan said with a trace of disappointment in his voice. "He's the only one who really appreciates superhero stuff as much as I do. It's nice having him around."

Matt grunted in reply. *Why couldn't that jerk just get his own friends?* Matt thought as he headed upstairs to the safety of his room.

Dan raced over to FalconTech. He knew they didn't care if he was late or not, but it was a matter of pride. He didn't really have that important of a job. Well, "job" was misleading, as that implied there was a salary. This was just an internship. The official title was Social Marketing Executive Assistant, which may have sounded impressive, but basically meant that Dan spent most of his time on social media sites like Twitter, Instagram, and Facebook, making posts for the company.

He stopped as he reached the FalconTech building, which loomed over him. It was a tall glass building, with the FalconTech logo on top. Dan often found himself gazing at it in awe. It truly was majestic. He checked his reflection in the glass wall before walking in, to make sure he was presentable. His blue button-down shirt had gotten loose. He tucked it back in as he walked inside.

Dan's job wasn't hard, and he often spent most of it in a little cubicle spacing out. This wasn't what he had in mind when he'd signed up. Dan expected he'd be working with engineers or something, preparing himself for a future career. Instead, he'd spend his time daydreaming of being a superhero, which admittedly was a fun distraction from real life. The longer he was at work, the longer it meant he wouldn't have to be home. And he was padding his resume, which didn't hurt.

He found it hard not to think about real life today though. Steve had humiliated him. *Well, why should today be any different?* Dan thought bitterly. At least Rose wasn't there to see his humiliation.

He sighed. Rose was gorgeous. She had flowing, silky black hair, small, deep-set eyes, these striking high cheekbones, and a killer body. Plus, she didn't seem as shallow as other girls. There seemed to be something more about her. Dan smiled to himself. Rose was his second favorite daydream. He'd speak to her eventually. He was just waiting for the right moment.

Dan was pretty sure Rose had noticed him looking at her in the cafeteria last week, so he made sure to be extra engrossed in his lunch this week to belay any suspicion. The thought crossed his mind that perhaps he was overreacting just a little.

The truth was, Dan didn't really know much about Rose. He *knew* that. He knew logically it didn't make sense to be obsessed with her. But that didn't stop him. He ran through the list in his head, checking off what he knew about her. She was hot, of course. And she liked to read. Regular books though, not comic books.

Oh, she would be just perfect if she liked comic books, Dan thought. I bet I could convince her, get her to like them.

He rolled his eyes at his own inner monologue. "Yeah, bet I could totally convince her," he mumbled sarcastically to himself. "I can't even talk to her."

What would she see in a guy like him anyway? A guy with only two friends. A loser who's never home because his parents are constantly fighting. A weakling who's constantly bullied. A coward who can't even work up the courage to walk up to her and say hello.

He leaned back in his chair, pondering what she thought of him. Does she think I'm a loser? Probably not, he decided. No, she doesn't think of me at all. She probably doesn't even know I exist. And somehow, that felt even worse.

CHAPTER EIGHT

It was dark by the time Dan got home. He'd finished work when it was still daylight, but he had taken a break on his way home to sit on a bench in the local park. He was in no hurry.

Dan stopped outside the door. He could hear voices, but couldn't make out what they were saying. There was a good chance it was just the TV.

He took a deep breath and walked in. It was dark. The only light came from the television, illuminating his mother, a gaunt woman with thin lips and large eyes who was passed out on the couch. There was a half-empty bottle of whiskey in her arms.

Dan sighed, dropping his backpack to the floor. His mother stirred as he took the bottle out of her arms and kissed her on her forehead. She mumbled incoherently. Dan placed the bottle on the dining room table and looked around. His father was nowhere to be seen. Dan wondered for a moment where he was before pushing the thought out of his head. He didn't *want* to know. He'd be happier this way.

Dan poured himself a bowl of cereal and sat down in front of his computer for dinner. He liked to browse superhero news websites while he ate. Someone had uploaded a cell phone video of Spark catching a guy. Dan watched the video and smiled.

He would make a great superhero, he thought. It would be so cool, and it would totally make up for all the garbage he had to go through. He laughed silently at his own thoughts. He couldn't even beat a high school bully. There was no way he could stop *real* supervillains.

There was a noise. Dan jerked awake. It sounded like a door slamming. He wiped the drool from his mouth and looked at his phone. It was six in the morning.

What could be making that racket?

Dan lifted himself out of bed, tiptoeing to the door. He opened the door a crack, to see his father stumbling down the hallway, eyes bloodshot.

Suddenly, there was a loud, shrill voice. "Where have you been all night?" Dan's mother yelled.

"I don't have to explain myself to you, woman!" his father responded irritably.

Dan closed his eyes and put his hands on his ears, hoping to drown out the noise. Hoping to wake up. Hoping for it all to be a dream. But when he opened his eyes and ears again, he was still there. His parents were still arguing, louder than ever. Dan sat on the carpet in silence for a few minutes, just listening, hoping it would end soon.

It didn't.

Dan reluctantly got up and scurried toward his closet, taking out a shirt. He was up anyway, might as well get dressed and leave to school early.

There was no way he was going to stick around for more of *this*.

CHAPTER NINE

When Matt arrived at school, Dan and Amy were already waiting. Even though Matt had known Amy far longer than Dan did, he sometimes felt a little left out of their morning conversations. Of course, that was partly his fault. He was late to school more often than he'd have liked. At this point, Matt was just happy he'd managed to arrive a little early. Dan and Amy were apparently discussing which superpowers they'd like to have, assuming they had a choice and superpowers actually existed.

"Hm. I don't know," Amy said, stroking her imaginary beard. "Mind reading, I guess."

Dan laughed. "Why would you want to know what people are thinking? It's all awful stuff, really."

"It's true," Matt chimed in. "I mean, maybe girls have decent thoughts, but you do *not* want to read a guy's mind, believe me."

Amy laughed. "What about you? If you could have one power, what power would you want to have?"

Matt thought for a moment. "Super speed." He chuckled. "Then I'd never be late!"

Amy smiled.

"What about you, Dan?" Matt asked.

"Flight. Just to be able to get out of here any time I wanted. To be able to go wherever, escape to anywhere, see the world from so high up. Untouchable. It's the ultimate freedom." Dan looked up at the sky wistfully.

Matt was about to crack a joke about Dan's head already being in the clouds, but thought better of it.

"Ooh! Flight sounds good. I'm switching mine to that one!" Amy said with a grin. "Although," she continued, "a more interesting question isn't what kind of powers you'd want, it's what would you do with them?"

Matt laughed. "We all know what Dan would do!"

Dan's ears turned red. "And you wouldn't be a superhero?"

Matt shook his head. "So I can go to an early grave? No thank you. I'd probably just use my powers for my own stuff. It's not like I'd be a supervillain or anything."

"Well I would," Amy interjected. Matt and Dan looked at Amy in shock. She was *far* too sweet to ever be a villain of any kind, super or otherwise. "I mean, if I took over the world, I could make it into a better place." She flashed a smile. "Just imagine, Empress Amy!" She put her hands on her hips as she looked at the two. "It has a nice ring to it."

Class was uneventful, for the most part. Matt was excited that they were nearing the end of the Civil War in his history class. The late 1800s had always been his favorite era of American history, before cars and the like showed up and ruined everything. Before city life exploded. He craved simpler times, although Dan would often remind him those times had their fair share of problems too.

By the time lunch came around, Matt was famished. This time, he ate the food he was served, despite not knowing what exactly it was. Amy spent the lunch period eating with other friends of hers, while Dan sat across from Matt pretending not to be looking at Rose, who was sitting on the other side of the room. Matt and Dan ate in silence for a time, before Matt finally broke it.

"Oh, just get up and talk to her!"

Dan raised his eyebrows. "What?"

"What are you waiting for? Just do it! All this sitting around and wondering, it's not doing you any good."

"I can't," Dan said, putting down his fork. "I mean, I can, I will, but not yet. I'm not ready."

"So when will you be?" Matt asked, the frustration heard clearly in his voice.

"It's not that simple," Dan replied. "If I ask her, there's a chance, a *good* chance, that she'll say 'no'. Then where will I be? At least like this, there's always the *possibility* she likes me."

"What? Yeah, but even if she says 'no,' then at least you can move on."

Dan nodded slowly. "I know. You're right. I know that. But I'm not ready to lose the chance that she might like me. Not yet."

Matt nodded. He understood. Sometimes it was better not to know.

CHAPTER TEN

There was a nondescript white van parked near the 34th Street Bank. Within the van was a robot and a man in a white lab coat, tapping his foot. The man in the lab coat checked to make sure the plastic-looking gun in his hand was properly calibrated. He looked at his robot in the driver's seat.

"Wish me luck, buddy."

The robot didn't respond. Alan Swift glanced at his watch. It was show time.

He slid open the side door and leaped out. His black combat boots hit the pavement. He squinted as the sunlight momentarily blinded him.

Alan didn't often do day heists. There was usually less of a chance of running into an actual superhero, and cops simply didn't offer the same challenge. The street was fairly crowded. There were gasps and points from onlookers as Alan Swift calmly strolled into the bank. He was pleasantly surprised that he was able to get a spot so close to it.

An overweight mustachioed officer was sitting on a chair by the door, reading a newspaper. He glanced up. Recognizing the Inventor, his eyes bulged as he jumped up from his seat, the chair clattering to the floor. The officer drew his gun, pointing it at the Inventor.

Alan chuckled. Well, now was as good a time as any to see just how smart he really was. Alan quickly raised the vibrational frequency gun and pulled the trigger. Having the setting rest on the vibrational frequency of metal caused the gun to shatter in the officer's hands into millions of tiny pieces, causing a loud noise.

Alan looked around. He had every person in the bank's attention now. The officer held his bloody hand. Alan winced as he glanced at it. *With some medical attention, the man'll be fine*, he told himself.

"Alright, everyone on the ground!" Alan yelled. "Now!"

Allan grinned as everyone listened. A whole bank full of people, as my audience, he thought excitedly. And the best kind of audience too. A captive audience.

"I'm the Inventor! Perhaps you've heard of me. Now if everyone listens, no one will get hurt."

He proceeded to laugh maniacally. It was a practiced laugh. He had hired a vocal coach to help him with it a few years back. After all, his audience deserved only the best.

"You there!" he said, pointing to an employee, a scared young girl, likely still in her twenties, clad in a white shirt and a vest. He glanced at her nametag. "Julie, be a dear and point me to the vault." She pointed behind her.

Alan began walking, then quickly stopped and turned around. There was a black-haired teenage boy on his cell phone.

"You!" he bellowed. The boy stopped and looked up, terror in his eyes. "Are you calling the police?"

"No, just recording all this. For my YouTube channel," he stammered.

"Oh," said Alan, surprised but pleased. "You got the laugh, right?"

The boy nodded meekly.

"Cool. Carry on."

Alan walked to the vault door, putting on his goggles. The door was huge, round, and looked unbreakable. It was probably ten inches thick, he surmised, and weighed at or around half a ton.

"Well the bigger they are..." he muttered, raising the vibrational frequency gun and pulling the trigger.

Nothing happened.

Alan looked at the gun, confused. Was it broken? He glanced at his watch. He only had about a minute more before the bank would be swarming with cops.

He wiped some sweat from his brow and aimed it again. This time when Alan pulled the trigger, he held it down. After a few seconds, there was a loud screeching noise, like metal rubbing against metal. The shrill noise grew louder and louder. The vault door began shaking. Alan backed away slowly.

Suddenly, the door exploded, shattering into millions of tiny metal shards. Silver dust filled the room.

Alan covered his mouth and nose with his sleeve as he walked through the dust cloud into the vault. There were piles of carefully stacked wads of green dollar bills, some piles as tall as a person. It was beautiful.

Alan whipped out a large white cloth bag from his coat pocket, with a carefully drawn dollar sign on its side, and proceeded to fill it with cash. After the bag was heavy enough, but not too heavy to carry, Alan swung it over his shoulder and calmly walked out.

Everyone was still lying on the floor in the lobby, looking terrified.

"Oh, calm down, fellas. I'm on my way out!" Alan said with a grin. He pointed to the boy with the phone out, recording everything. "You there, what's your name?"

The boy didn't answer for a minute, as though he was watching someone else's conversation, and wasn't aware anyone was actually talking to him. Finally, his eyes snapped up with a sudden realization.

"Um, Jerry?" he answered, sounding unsure.

Alan looked into the phone's lens. "Hey, there, it's the Inventor! I'm here on Jerry's YouTube channel. Remember to like and subscribe!" He flashed his best smile.

Jerry's eyes lit up. His mouth opened to say something, but no sound came out.

Alan cocked his head. He could hear something. It was faint, but getting louder.

Sirens.

He had taken too long. He raced out of the bank and toward the white van. The side door swung open as he approached. Alan jumped in.

"Drive!" he yelled as he closed the door. The car began driving.

"There is an error," said the robot as it drove. "The GPS is having trouble connecting."

"Again!?!" Alan exclaimed in disbelief. No, that's not entirely true. He *could* believe it.

I really should learn how to drive myself, he thought. Though who actually drives in New York?

Alan looked out the front window. A cop car, its lights flashing, was blocking the road.

"Oh, for Roddenberry's sake!" he exclaimed.

Alan, still sitting in the back of the van, lifted the vibrational frequency gun and pulled the trigger, holding it down. The police car in front of them began shaking, then exploded in a silvery mist.

Alan's eyes opened wide when he realized the van was shaking too. Adrenalin pumping through him, he scrambled to the side door, swung it open, and dived out. He could hear the van explode behind him. The robot is likely destroyed as well, he thought with a frown as he tumbled onto the street. He looked up to see four officers racing toward him.

No! The Inventor doesn't get caught, he thought frantically.

Alan grabbed at his back. Luckily, he was still wearing his jetpack. He breathed a sigh of relief as he turned it on and took to the air just as the officers were closing in. As Alan looked down at the ground falling away, he realized he had dropped the vibrational frequency gun when he dove out of the van.

He looked back, just as a bullet whizzed by his nose, and felt the air brush past his face. It was *far* too close for comfort. There was no time to worry about the gun. He had to get someplace safe before the NYPD sent out their helicopters.

I should've planned this better, he thought, kicking himself. It was not one of his best performances. *At least it was an entertaining one,* he thought with a sigh.

CHAPTER ELEVEN

After the final bell, Matt, Dan, and Amy met up in front of the school before heading off on their separate ways.

"Hey, so there's some sort of a bank robbery going on in the city right now," Dan said, looking down at his smartphone.

Matt never had much of an interest in the news or current events. If not for Dan, he probably wouldn't know anything that was going on beyond his own line of vision.

"It's the Inventor. You know, the supervillain?"

Matt shook his head. The name sounded familiar, and he was pretty sure he'd heard it before, but he just didn't really follow the whole superhero/supervillain thing.

"Oh, yeah," Amy said nodding. "Wasn't he the guy who tried to make it look like the Statue of Liberty was holding a gun instead of a torch?"

Matt remembered now. It was all over the news last year. The media figured it was some sort of a political statement or something. The Inventor had denied it in an online statement, claiming it was just funny.

"So are there any superheroes there?" Matt asked, trying to contribute to the conversation. "You know, trying to stop him?"

Dan shook his head. "No, it doesn't say anything about that here. I mean, I suppose Spark or Dragonfly could show up, but it is daytime, so that's fairly unlikely."

"Hm," was all Matt could reply.

"Eh, I'm sure he'll be caught," Amy said dismissively. "I mean, all supervillains eventually are. Unless I become one of course," she added with a chuckle.

"Actually," Dan began, "not necessarily. Quite a few supervillains were never caught, and the Inventor has been around nearly ten years and still hasn't seen the inside of a prison cell."

"He'll get caught eventually," Amy said again, confidently.

"Um, I think Dan's right," Matt interjected. Amy shot him a look. "I mean, most crimes in the United States are never solved, I think. I'm sure I read that somewhere."

"Yeah, whatever, I gotta go," Amy said, showing her slight annoyance.

"Same here," said Dan. "I've got work."

Matt nodded, and saw the two of them run off.

Matt trudged home from school alone. Ever since Dan got that internship and Amy got a little brother, walking home alone became the norm. As he arrived at his house, he noticed his mother, Marilyn, had her car parked in the ridiculously narrow driveway.

What's she doing home so early? Matt wondered.

She'd already started her new job. Maybe he'd be able to take the car out, he thought. Despite having his license for over a month, his parents still didn't let him use the car. He was sure he'd wear them down eventually. It's not like they had a good reason for not letting him. *Anyone* could've broken off that mirror while pulling out of their narrow driveway.

By the time he'd entered the house, Matt had already begun mentally preparing his three-pronged speech explaining why he should be allowed to borrow the car.

"Mom?" he yelled as he walked in.

"She's not here," Evan said as he came down the stairs. Matt frowned. "She took the train today. Left me the car."

"What? Why?"

Evan smiled wide. "I'm meeting a lady tonight."

Matt scowled. "What time are you going to be home?"

"I might be pretty late," Evan said grinning as he wiggled his eyebrows.

Matt rolled his eyes. "Just try to be quiet when you get home. And stay out of my room!"

Matt stomped up the stairs, shoving Evan with his shoulder as he passed him.

Evan laughed. "Aw, Matty, you're still upset about the iPad thing? That was days ago!"

"I'm not talking to you!" Matt yelled from the top of the stairs.

Evan chuckled.

Matt sneered at him. That jerk never apologized when he did something wrong. Matt walked into his room and slammed the door. He seethed with anger. Why did Even always do this to him, Matt wondered. And why did he let him?

As Matt sat on the bed and closed his eyes. He reminded himself to take deep breaths.

In, out. In, out.

A knock on his door interrupted his meditation.

"Matty, you there?" Evan asked from the other side of the door.

"Go away."

There was silence for a few seconds, before Evan spoke again. "Well, I'm not leaving until a little later." He sighed. "I can take you driving if you want."

Matt couldn't believe his ears. He jumped up, darted to the door, and opened it. "Really?"

Evan stood in the doorway and smiled. "Really."

He threw Matt the keys.

CHAPTER TWELVE

Matt's eyes opened slowly. His vision was blurry, taking longer than it should have to come into focus. There was a sharp pain in his right leg. He must've bumped it against something. His hands grabbed his chest. It felt as though it had just been punched.

What the heck happened?

There was smoke everywhere, seemingly coming from the airbag directly in front of him, along with an acrid smell he could not describe. Later he'd be told he had inhaled gunpowder, which was commonly used to inflate airbags.

A dull throbbing ache in Matt's head was causing it to ring. He put his hand to his forehead.

Wet.

A quick glance confirmed it was blood. He saw through the smoke. The windshield was shattered. A few pieces of glass littered the dashboard. With a jolt of adrenalin, Matt remembered Evan.

He strained as he turned his head to his right, finding his brother stirring in the passenger's seat. It appeared Evan was trying to say something, but Matt couldn't hear him. He couldn't understand why. Suddenly it occurred to Matt that there was music playing. The engine was still running. Matt quickly reached over and pulled out the key, finally silencing the music and allowing him to make out his brother's words.

"...Matt? I'm sorry, I don't know how..." Evan's eyes opened weakly. He seemed to be struggling to stay conscious.

Why is he sorry? Matt thought. *I was driving.* "Don't talk," he said quickly, "We'll be fine. I think I can hear sirens."

Evan didn't seem to hear him. His eyes had closed. "If I don't... It's under the bed. Have to... return... Carry... legacy..."

Matt was confused. His head was pounding. Hard to think.

"I promise," he said, not sure what he was promising, or if Evan could even hear him.

Evan tried to say something else, but it came out as a gurgle.

As the car doors opened, light flooded in. Matt was dragged from the car, the smell of gunpowder forever etched in his brain.

CHAPTER THIRTEEN

Matt and Evan went to the hospital in different ambulances. Try as he might, Matt couldn't remember the accident itself. Only its aftermath. And the smell of gunpowder. He would later be told that he was speeding when he lost control of the car and collided with a concrete barrier. While in the ambulance, Matt realized that he had taken Evan's phone from the charger when they had been pulled out of the car. The rest of the ride to the hospital entailed Matt insisting to the EMT that he had to get the phone back to Evan. It seemed incredibly important to him, although he wasn't sure why.

Matt was wheeled in on a bed and asked to fill out paperwork while he waited for the doctor to arrive. A somewhat pushy, overweight nurse asked him about what happened, how his head felt, was there anything that hurt him, and how hurt he felt on a scale from one to ten. They weren't hard questions, but Matt found himself having a difficult time answering them. She left to get the doctor, leaving Matt alone for what felt like an eternity.

Finally, the doctor showed up, only to ask Matt the same questions the nurse asked. Matt should've felt frustrated, but he was too tired.

"Hey, how's my brother doing?" Matt asked weakly. "I came in with him?"

The doctor didn't seem to take any notice. "So we're going to have to run x-rays and a CAT scan, is that alright?"

After what seemed like an eternity of being wheeled from scan to scan and test to test, though mostly waiting around in an uncomfortable bed, staring at the ceiling, Matt was finally told that barring a possible concussion, a cut on his forehead, and a few bruises, he was fine. As the doctor delivered the news, Marilyn Stone walked into the room.

"Oh, Matt, thank goodness you're alright!" she said as she hugged Matt. "Oh, my baby! My little Matty!"

Matt smiled, despite the pain. "Yeah, I'm okay, Ma," he said. "Where's Dad?"

"Oh, he's with Evan." She said. Marilyn's voice cracked. It seemed like she was trying to hold back tears, although Matt didn't seem to notice.

"How's Evan doing? The doctors here won't tell me anything." He lifted up the phone. "Here's Evan's phone, can you give it to him?"

Marilyn's face betrayed that she was clearly in pain. After what seemed like too long a moment of trying to hold it in, she burst out crying as she hugged Matt again.

The first feeling Matt felt was an intense sense of discomfort. It's always uncomfortable for a child to see a parent cry. Then a wave a dread passed over Matt.

"Mom, is he okay?" he asked urgently. "Is Evan okay?"

Marilyn didn't answer. She didn't have to. She just held her son and continued to sob.

CHAPTER FOURTEEN

There was nothing quite like reading the reviews of his most recent performance in the morning's paper. Of course, Alan read them on his tablet. No one read actual newspapers anymore. Plus, reading it online meant he wouldn't have to leave the house.

He was still wearing his lab coat—he hadn't bothered taking it off the day before, although he did change into his sweatpants. He didn't plan on going out today anyway, so he reasoned he'd spend the rest of the day dressed like that.

Alan poured himself a mug of hot cocoa. He wasn't really a coffee person. Oh, he tried, when he was just a young college student at MIT, but he could never seem to acquire the taste for it. The steam from the hot cocoa rose, warming his face as it dispersed around him. He sipped slowly as he read, careful not to burn his tongue. The article read:

THE INVENTOR FLEES IN
BOTCHED ROBBERY ATTEMPT

Alan Swift, better known as "The Inventor," a well-known, if small-time supervillain, was unsuccessful when he attempted to rob the 34th

Street Bank yesterday. The Inventor is a staple of New York City with his monthly, often public, outlandish crimes. While the attempt was unusual for the Inventor in that it took place during the day, it was not unusual in that it failed. This time, however, the Inventor was foiled not by local superheroes Spark or Dragonfly, but rather by New York's Finest. Although the Inventor escaped, the high-tech weapon used in the daring robbery attempt was recovered at the scene and is currently in the hands of the NYPD. Two officers were injured as a result of the event, and are currently being treated at New York Presbyterian. They are expected to make a full recovery. One of the witnesses in the bank, Jerry Cho, recorded his ordeal...

There was more to the article, but Alan stopped reading. He never meant to injure anyone. *At least they're expected to make a full recovery*, he thought with relief.

There was a video clip embedded in the article. It was the footage taken by that Jerry kid. That meant even more people could enjoy his performance. All in all, he was pleased. He leaned back in his chair, content.

There was still work to be done, of course. He knew he would have to get the vibrational frequency device prototype back from the police evidence lockup somehow.

The phone rang. Alan cringed. Never a moment of peace. He gulped down the rest of his hot cocoa— it had gotten nearly lukewarm anyhow— and picked up the phone.

"Yes?"

"I caught your demonstration yesterday on the internet," the client said. "It was wonderful. So I guess the device works. Thank you."

The Inventor grinned from ear to ear. There was no better feeling than being complimented on your performance. "Oh, it was nothing. So how can I help you?"

"I was wondering if you can make an app to trigger the device remotely. Is that possible?"

Alan hesitated for a second. What could the client be working on? Why would he want this? No, it wasn't his place to ask questions. He was just the inventor, after all. Besides, he was fairly sure he wouldn't like the answer.

"Certainly," he responded. "Everything is possible for a price."

"I've already let you know money isn't an object," the client said, a trace of annoyance in his voice. "Make me one as soon as you're able. You'll be handsomely rewarded."

"Will do," Alan said as he hung up.

He slumped back in his chair and sighed, trying to stifle his curiosity as to what his inventions would be used for. He already sent two men to the hospital with this particular invention. Was he really going to be responsible for whatever his client had planned? He'd built dangerous devices for clients before, but nothing with as much destructive capability as this one.

He wondered how Wernher von Braun must've felt when he created the German V-2 rocket in World War II. Alan recalled von Braun was quoted, likely inaccurately, saying, "I aim at the stars, but sometimes I hit London."

It was true that the man had done good work in his life, such as working for NASA to help make landing on the moon possible, but he was also responsible for so many deaths. Heck, he was a Nazi.

Alan pondered where *his* name would fall in history. The point of entertaining others is to be remembered, isn't it? That's a large reason why Alan performs. That's why writers write and artists paint. Because of an innate drive, sure, but also to be remembered. To be made immortal by existing in the thoughts of others long after leaving the world behind. A legacy. And Alan wouldn't be remembered as a monster. Not like von Braun.

Alan groaned in frustration. He was getting a headache. Quantum mechanics were easy, but philosophy and subjective truth? Alan didn't handle those well at all. He pushed the thoughts out of his mind. No, he had made a deal, and he was going to deliver. The Inventor was a man of his word.

Whatever the client does with it will be on his head, not mine, he concluded.

Alan's ears perked up as he heard a distinct ping. He opened his laptop enthusiastically, knowing what that ping meant. A new email was waiting for him. His eyes scanned the screen eagerly as he read the email with excitement. Finally, a new client.

"Build a safe device that produces a localized electromagnetic pulse?" he muttered to himself excitedly. "That would be a challenge."

And a challenge was just what he needed to take his mind off what had been plaguing him. As he ran to the blackboard and began to work, he tried to push all irrelevant thoughts out of his mind. However there was one terrorizing thought that, try as he might, he couldn't expel: *Am I growing a conscience?*

CHAPTER FIFTEEN

Amy hadn't seen Matt since Evan's funeral, which had taken place a few days before. She had called the house a few times, but rarely did anyone pick up, and when someone did, it wasn't Matt.

After school that day she walked over to visit him. Amy wondered if the red-and-white shirt and short blue skirt she was wearing was appropriate when visiting a house in mourning. She wondered if she should have worn black, as she took out her hairband, letting her coffee-colored hair cascade down onto her shoulders. She was sure a ponytail wasn't appropriate.

As she walked down the block, Amy noted the weather was gorgeous and sunny, just as it had been the day of Evan's funeral. The birds were chirping, drowning out the sound of the crickets, the grass was green and the sky was blue. Amy remembered thinking how inappropriate it seemed, life going on all around when it felt everything should've stopped. A funeral was no place for nice weather.

As she approached the house, she noticed the door was open, with people going in and out freely. It was silly to think she would be the only one visiting.

Upon entering, Amy noticed most of the people were neighbors or friends of Matt's parents. The walls were covered with pictures of Evan, most of which seemed recently put up. The table was covered with flowers, cards, and freshly baked food brought over by well-wishers.

She looked around at the people in the room, most of whom she didn't recognize. Matt was nowhere to be seen. Matt's father was in the middle of telling a funny story about Evan to a captive crowd.

She felt a little uncomfortable as she stood in the corner, unsure of her place among the gathering. It was times like these that made Amy wonder about what would be said of her when her time came. Amy hoped they'd say good things about her. She hoped she'd have made enough of a difference in people's lives that it would matter to them when she was gone. Amy shivered at the macabre thoughts running through her head. There was a tap on her shoulder.

"Amy, thank you for coming," Marilyn said, a kind smile upon her face.

"Hey, Mrs. Stone, how're you doing?" Amy searched Marilyn's face, seeing if she could detect the mask she was wearing, trying to hide her pain.

"I've told you, Mrs. Stone is my mother-in-law. Call me Marilyn," she said, a kind smile still on her face, though it was slowly becoming more apparent that it was fake. "Matt's upstairs."

"Thanks," Amy said, about to head up before pausing. "I'm sorry for your loss. I really liked Evan. He was an amazing guy."

Mrs. Stone began tearing up and nodded.

Amy reached Matt's room. She was about to knock before realizing the door was already slightly ajar.

"Matt?" she said as she opened the door.

Clothes were strewn all over the room, to the point that it was hard to make out the floor. There was a half-eaten sandwich on the desk, along with a crumbled-up napkin and a nearly-empty cup of some sort of cola. Matt was sitting on his bed, his feet folded atop each other, reading a book. He looked up, his eyes looked dark and sunken in.

"Oh, hey Amy," he said as he put down the book. "Sorry I wasn't downstairs. I just can't, y'know, it just..."

Matt fell silent. His blond hair was a mess, as though it hadn't been combed or brushed in days, and his face looked sticky, with a few new acne breakouts. Amy suspected it had been a while since he last showered.

Poor thing, she thought. *He probably blames himself.* Amy tried to push the thought out of her mind. She knew Matt wouldn't appreciate being pitied, which was admittedly a challenge, seeing Matt in this state.

Amy sat down next to him and put her hand on his back. "I know, I know," she whispered. "It's a lot."

Matt nodded. Amy held Matt's hand, and their fingers intertwined. Matt and Amy sat there in silence for several minutes. Amy cleared her throat, still unsure of what to say, but feeling the need to break the silence.

"So, um, Dan's sorry he couldn't make it."

Matt looked at her blankly.

"He's, um, going through some stuff," she added, knowing no excuse would really be good enough to excuse him. "It turns out his parents are finally getting a divorce."

"That sucks," Matt replied.

Amy nodded, not sure if Matt was talking about Dan's parents' divorce or Dan not visiting. She felt as though she was suddenly over-analyzing everything. Amy liked to consider herself empathetic, knowing exactly how to react in social situations. She wasn't used to feeling so useless.

Matt suddenly started sobbing. It was an unsettling, rhythmic noise. Amy felt very uncomfortable. She hadn't seen Matt cry since he was ten. She wasn't sure how she was supposed to react. Amy found herself wrapping her arms around him, hugging him, trying to make out the words he was saying between sobs.

"I miss him. I feel like it should've been me. Why wasn't it me?" He looked up at her with his bloodshot eyes, as if she had the answer. "I mean, I was driving. It's all my fault. Why wasn't it me?"

Amy's heart broke. She took a clean tissue out of her pocket and handed it to him.

Matt blew his nose and looked down at the dirty tissue, analyzing it as if it contained the solution to every problem in the universe, before shaking his head and throwing the tissue in the waste basket.

Amy looked at him, not sure what to say. She found herself tearing up. "I don't know why this happened. I don't know what to tell you to make you feel better," she said, honestly. "I wish I did."

Matt began crying again and hugged her.

Amy kissed his forehead and held him. She understood at that moment that was all she could do.

CHAPTER SIXTEEN

Every night for the past week the dream had been the same. Well, similar, anyway. Details varied. They would always be driving though, either down a twisting country road, down a city street, or on a bridge. Depending on the night, sometimes Evan would be driving, sometimes Matt. The ending was always the same. The deafening thud, the breaking glass, and the bitter smell of gunpowder.

Matt awoke with a start. He sat up, breathing heavily, drenched in sweat. He glanced at the clock. The red neon numbers informed him it was far earlier than he'd have liked.

Matt sighed and turned over, trying to go back to sleep. Suddenly he snapped up. In the madness of the past week, he had forgotten what Even told him, and the promise he had made.

Matt closed his eyes, trying to remember. *The bed!* He thought, eyes shooting open. *Evan told me to check under his bed!*

Matt stealthily crept out of his room, careful not to wake his parents. There was no way he would be going back to sleep tonight. As he entered Evan's room, undisturbed since his passing, Matt cautiously closed the door. He neared the bed, and dropped to his knees, reaching below the bed. His hands touched something that felt like leather. Matt pulled out the leather trunk. It was big, about the size of a large desktop computer.

Locked! Matt thought in frustration, as he futilely tried to open it.

Matt sat, looking at the trunk. It was almost as if it was taunting him. Evan had said this trunk was his legacy. What did he mean? And where would he leave the key?

Matt's eyes opened wide as the realization hit him. He jumped up and hurried over to Evan's desk. After a minute of rummaging, he found it. It was Evan's old lock picking set. Matt began working on the lock.

Seven minutes had passed, and Matt was losing his patience. Lock picking didn't take mere seconds, like it did in the movies.

Had Evan always spent ten minutes trying to break into my room every time he tried to prank me or take my stuff? Matt thought, as he imagined Evan spending all that time breaking in just trying to put a rubber spider on Matt's bed. He chuckled, then immediately felt guilty.

More time passed, and it seemed like Matt was getting nowhere. He sighed, just about to give up, when he heard a faint *click*. With bated breath, he opened the trunk.

The inside of the trunk contained a few journals, a few flash drives, a small flashlight, and something else.

Matt's breath got caught in his throat. He realized the truth behind his brother's secret. It explained *everything*.

At first it looked like a costume someone would wear on Halloween or Purim. He lifted up the suit. It was black, with blue highlights and a blue "S" logo on the chest. It had a leathery feel, but was able to stretch as well. Certain areas appeared to be armored, and there looked like there was a charging cord that connected to a port on one of the attached boots.

Matt lifted up the costume. As a whole, the suit was heavier than it looked. He took out the first journal and held it with reverence.

This was Evan's legacy. Evan was a superhero. And not just any superhero.

Evan was Spark.

Matt spent the rest of the night reading through Evan's journals. The journals described how Evan had gotten his hands on the suit, how he had chosen a name (he wanted to be a "spark of hope"), and described his various adventures over the past year.

Spark had fought a few costumed villains, most notably The Inventor and The Pyromaniac, small-time criminals that Dan would've referred to as "C-list villains." Most of the entries involved random drug dealers and the like, and a few robberies that were stopped. There as an entry about a rogue circus performer in a flashy circus costume which Matt found humorous.

Matt noted how very few of Spark's adventures made the news, yet obviously enough of them did to make Spark the most popular superhero in the city. Although considering his only other competition was Dragonfly, it didn't seem like much of an accomplishment.

There was a newspaper clipping taped onto one of the pages with one of the rare photographs of Spark, holding a baby he'd just saved from a burning building. Apparently Evan thought the Pyromaniac was involved somehow, according to the writing on the opposite page.

As Matt started reaching the end of the journals, he began to realize that being a superhero had started to take a toll on Evan. He seemed to get more paranoid with each page. At one point he even suspected he was being followed. He entertained the idea that someone might have discovered his secret identity and was possibly trying to kill or expose him.

This didn't surprise Matt. Superheroes didn't have long lifespans, and he couldn't understand why someone would willingly choose to become one. The thought crossed Matt's mind, that maybe Evan's death was somehow a murder. Perhaps someone, a supervillain or the like, cut the brakes or something. If someone sabotaged the car in an attempt to kill Spark, that would mean that Matt wasn't responsible for Evan's death. But if that was the case, who was?

The thought was interrupted as a piece of paper fell out from between the pages. Matt picked it up and read it.

If you're reading this, it probably means I'm gone. But that doesn't mean Spark is dead. Spark is my legacy, and the world will always need a spark of hope. The suit is yours, assuming it's still in the chest. Please keep Spark alive.

Matt read the note over and over. He expected a signature at the end, and was almost disappointed there wasn't one. That's how Matt would've written it. By the time he finished reading the note for the sixth time, Matt knew he didn't have a choice. He had made a promise to his dying brother, and now he had to keep it.

Matt knew logically this would eventually mean his death. Few heroes ever make it beyond the two year mark. But that didn't matter, he thought as he held up the suit, studying it. He had made a promise, and knew he could never live with himself if he didn't at least try to keep it. He owed Evan that much. In his mind, the matter was settled.

Matt Stone was going to become Spark.

CHAPTER SEVENTEEN

School was torture; more so than usual. Matt couldn't concentrate on anything. He couldn't wait for the final bell to ring, for night to fall, to try on the suit. Some say time is subjective, moving faster or slower depending on the actions or desires of a person and the brain's perception, but Matt never believed it before that day. A minute seemed to last an hour. An hour seemed to last a week.

He shivered. Someone had decided to crank the air conditioning up to combat the heat outside, making the classrooms feel like a freezer.

When will this cruelty end? He wondered as he played the previous evening over and over in his head. Matt was unsure what bothered him more, the cold or the knowledge that the Spark suit was back at home, waiting for him.

Matt's eyes darted toward the clock. The ticking of the second hand seemed to be getting exponentially slower. He felt like it was taunting him. Matt tried to concentrate on the lesson, but it was no use. Nothing could take his mind off the suit.

At one point he glanced at the timepiece and could swear the hands were moving backwards. By the time his lunch period had arrived, Matt had felt as though months had passed.

"Matt? Are you feeling okay?" Amy asked worriedly.

"Hm?" Matt looked up from busily moving his peas from one side of the plate to the other. Amy's concerned face stared back across from him. "I'm fine."

Amy's brow furrowed. "I'm not going to pretend I know what you're going through, but if you need anyone to talk to..."

"I'm fine. Really," said Matt, but his facial expressions betrayed his words.

Dan sat down next to Matt. "Hey man. You okay?"

Matt was annoyed. What the heck was it with everyone asking him irritating questions? "I'm fine!" he snapped. "Are you ok with your parent's divorce?"

The second the words left Matt's lips, he regretted them. He wished there was a way to somehow stop the sound waves from reaching Dan's ears. But the damage was done. Dan looked hurt. His eyes looked like they were about to water.

Dan's face quickly flashed from shock and hurt to anger. "What the heck?" Dan yelled.

Matt had never seen him so upset before. Dan gave Matt a look of hate and disgust that Matt would never forget, then shoved his lunch tray away and stormed off.

Amy kicked Matt under the table and shot him an angry look, making him feel worse than he felt already.

Matt turned in Dan's direction and opened his mouth, trying to apologize, but no sound came out. He felt ashamed. So instead, Matt just got up and left, and spent the rest of lunch wallowing in self-pity, sitting on the stoop in front of the school. With his mind distracted from the suit, the rest of the school day seemed to fly by.

By evening, Matt had taken the coward's way out and texted Dan an apology. He felt too embarrassed to do it in person or over the phone. Dan hadn't replied, and honestly, Matt couldn't blame him. He knew he had crossed a line.

Matt wondered how Evan would handle the situation pondering if Evan would've apologized in person.

No, he would've probably handled it the same way, by sending a text. Then again, Matt realized, that could be why Evan didn't have many friends, as far as he knew.

Matt reached under his bed for the trunk, determined to wash away lingering doubts and feelings. He took out one of Evan's journals, and lost himself in it for the next hour or so.

As soon as night had fallen and his parents were asleep, Matt was ready. He put on Evan's Spark suit for the first time. Evan was a little taller and broader than Matt, but thanks to the stretchy material, the suit still had a snug fit. As he put the mask over his head, he looked in the mirror. Matt was awestruck.

He looked like a superhero.

Oh, he wasn't overly muscled or whatever, but the padding seemed to give the impression. The light shined off the tight, leathery material. There was an opening on the top of the mask, where Matt's blond hair stuck out. Matt instantly thought of the risk of leaving his DNA everywhere if a stray hair were to fall out, before reminding himself that his DNA isn't in any criminal databases or the like. The gloves were textured, and it seemed like it would be easy to pick things up. He tried picking up a book. The gloves gripped easily.

Matt closed the trunk and pushed it under his bed. There was a thud as it slammed against the wall. Matt was surprised at how light it seemed. Apparently, the suit made him stronger, he gathered, as he looked at his hands, trying to figure out how it worked.

Matt brushed his hair out of his face, touching the side of his head, when suddenly everything changed. His vision turned green and obnoxiously bright. Night vision, he realized with excitement. He touched the spot on the mask again and his vision returned to normal.

Now it was time to try out the last thing, which both excited and scared Matt. He opened the window and stepped outside. Standing on the window's edge, he pushed and turned the Spark logo on the belt until he had heard a little click.

He jumped off the ledge, praying Evan's journals were accurate and not some elaborate joke. The ground shot up at him as he clicked his feet together, then stopped suddenly just before he hit the pavement.

Matt breathed a sigh of relief as he began rising. The ground fell away as Matt looked up. He could see the moon ahead of him. The air was crisp. Matt smiled. He was flying.

Matt looked down and began shifting direction. The houses looked as big as matchboxes from so high up. As he slowly spread his feet slightly apart, he began to gradually drop. After a few minutes, he learned that slight movements in his feet and head controlled direction, speed, and altitude. It surprisingly didn't take long to get the hang of.

As Matt flew beyond Brooklyn Heights, with the Brooklyn Bridge to his right, he lowered himself to just above the water, allowing his hand to skim it. Matt then shot up, vertically, the wind billowing in his face. Matt landed on a skyscraper and looked down at the city. For the first time since the accident, he couldn't help but smile.

Flying was like nothing he had ever experienced, and nothing could possibly describe just what if felt like. Words were meaningless. Flying felt like freedom. When hanging up there, for just a moment, everything else melted away. There was only Matt and the sky.

CHAPTER EIGHTEEN

Dan sat with Amy in the cafeteria. After what Matt had said the other day, it wasn't surprising he wasn't there. Dan had gotten a text the night before, as if a simple text could fix everything. Dan needed Matt to apologize personally. Sincerely.

"I still can't believe he said that! What a jerk!" Dan fumed.

Amy shifted in her seat uncomfortably. "I know. It was stupid of him. I'm sure he feels bad."

"He has a funny way of showing it," Dan muttered under his breath. He and Matt had avoided each other throughout classes and in the hallways.

"Hey look, It's Rose!" Amy said, trying to change the subject with all the subtlety of an elephant.

Dan turned his head, craning his neck. Yep, there she was. Rose was wearing her black leather jacket, her long silky black hair cascading down over it. She wore a liberal amount of lipstick and eyeliner. Most people would think it was too much for a girl her age, but Dan found it striking.

Man, she's hot, he thought.

Dan turned back to Amy. "I *will* ask her out, you know."

"I'm sure," Amy said dryly.

"I *will*! It's just that I'm still in the planning stages. I think I'm a good, oh, month or two away from actual audible contact."

Amy giggled. "Oh, just ask her out! What's the worst that could happen?"

"She says no, I become crushed and live out the rest of my days as a social outcast with her and her friends laughing at me every chance they get." He paused, thinking. "And then she kills me horribly," he added, "*after* months of torture." Clearly, he had thought too much about this. "Yeah, so that's the worst that could happen."

"Should I just talk to her?" Amy asked. "I can ask her out for you, or just see what she thinks of you."

"NO!" Dan shouted, alarmed.

A few people looked in their direction. Dan looked around, embarrassed. He noticed Matt was looking at him from across the room. The second their eyes met, both turned away. Dan noticed Matt looked depressed.

Good. He deserved to be.

Looking back at Amy, Dan said, "That's basically the worst thing you can do. What girl would go out with a guy who couldn't even ask her out?"

"What, are you scared she's gonna think you're a wimp?" Amy asked, her eyes narrowing, a sly smile forming at the edges of her mouth.

"Yes," Dan answered. "Yes I am."

"Then just stop being a wimp and do it."

"I *can't*."

Amy groaned loudly. "Well if you don't, I will."

Dan looked at Amy in shock. She *wouldn't*, would she? He studied her face, but it betrayed nothing. No, she probably wouldn't, he thought. She's too sweet. But on the slight chance he was wrong...

"Fine," Dan said, standing up. "But if I end up tortured and dead, that's on *your* head."

Amy giggled. "I'll live."

Rose was sitting down with her lunch in front of her, though she wasn't eating it. She was absorbed in a paperback book she was holding. As Dan walked toward her, his heart began to pound furiously. His throat began to dry up, and he found himself swallowing over and over to compensate. He clenched his hands into fists to keep them from shaking.

When he was a few feet away, something hit his side. Dan felt a sharp pain as he hit the ground. A few other kids chuckled. He looked up to find Steve looking down at him.

"Hey, stupid, watch where you're going!" Steve yelled at him.

Jerk.

Dan mumbled a halfhearted apology as he lifted himself off the floor, his face red. He looked at Rose, who was still in her book. Good. She hadn't seen anything. Steve's eyes followed Dan's gaze.

"Rose?" he whispered into Dan's ear as his tone became more menacing. "Don't you know she's *my* girl?"

Dan looked at him in shocked silence. Rose was Steve's girlfriend? No, that just didn't make sense. How could a jerk like Steve even get a girl? Much less a girl like Rose.

Steve shot Dan a look and shoved him out of the way as he walked past.

Dan felt nothing. He was still having trouble processing what he had just heard as he watched Steve sit down next to Rose and say something to her. Rose rolled her eyes.

They're probably talking about me, having a good laugh, Dan thought as his heart sunk. He sullenly walked back to Amy and just shrugged.

"Hey, what happened? Are you okay?" Amy asked.

"I don't want to talk about it," Dan grumbled.

The look she gave him was a look of pity. That was the worst. Dan hated feeling like this. Pathetic and annoying. Lately, he'd been such a downer.

Dan began to worry Amy wouldn't hang out with him anymore if he wasn't fun to hang out with, but he didn't know how to just change like that. How can someone just turn on the 'happy switch' in their brain?

He lowered his gaze to his food. He'd lost his appetite. Dan glanced up at Amy again, before turning away quickly. He hated seeing the look she gave him.

The bell rang. Thank goodness. Dan tersely said goodbye to Amy and headed to class.

Dan rushed outside as soon as the final bell rang. The less he was in school, the less of a chance he had to run into Matt or Steve. He walked down the street at a brisk pace, headed toward his internship at FalconTech.

There was a voice behind him. "Dan, wait up!" Amy ran over, slightly out of breath.

"I'm going to work now," Dan said quickly. He didn't feel like talking to anyone at the moment. And it was actually true. He *did* have to get to work.

"I'm going in that direction anyway. I promised my mother I'd pick up Marty after school."

"Alright," Dan said shrugging.

Amy liked to talk about her little brother Marty a lot. There was a huge age gap between the two. The kid was still a toddler, and it could honestly be annoying to hear Amy gush about him. He was really cute though.

"So, do you want to talk about it?" Amy asked. That's exactly what Dan was afraid of.

"Talk about what?" he said, playing stupid.

"Anything, I don't know."

But Dan did know. She wanted to talk about Matt. "I'm not talking about Matt."

"I'm sure he's sorry. You *know* he's sorry."

"Amy," Dan said, getting upset. "If he's so sorry, he should come over to me and apologize, like any decent human would. And even if he did, I don't know if I'd forgive him. You heard what he said!" Dan could feel the anger building inside him.

"I know," she said, looking down. "I'm not trying to defend him. He was wrong. I'm sure he knows that. He's probably too prideful to admit it."

"So I should just forgive him? Act like everything's okay? He's been avoiding me too!"

"I know, I know. It's just... I don't know. He's going through a hard time right now. That doesn't make what he did okay, but he did just lose a brother. And he was the one driving. He probably feels responsible. We can't imagine what he's going through."

Dan felt his anger fade. "I know. There are times I'm so upset, I'm burning, because of what he said. It was just..." He paused as he searched for the right word. "Soulless," he said finally. "But then when I think of what he's been going through, I feel so guilty for being upset at him." He looked at Amy questioningly. "I have a right to be angry, don't I? I mean, he was wrong."

Amy sighed. "Yeah, he shouldn't have said that." She paused for a moment, as if pondering whether or not she should say next what was on her mind. "But you never even called him since the funeral, and—"

"I know," Dan said, cutting her off. "I should have, I know. I was thinking of my own problems. But Matt is, well, *was* my friend. I should have visited him anyway. He'd have done it for me."

"He's *still* your friend," Amy said. "You guys are just going through a rough patch."

"Well, *you're* my best friend at the moment. My *only* one, really." He paused, unsure if he wanted to say this next part, knowing it would let Amy down. "I'm still not going to apologize to Matt until he apologizes to me, in person." Dan knew he still deserved at least that. "I mean, I may not have done something I should have, but he did something he *shouldn't* have. *I'm* the real wronged party here."

"*Guys,*" Amy said as she rolled her eyes. "And they say girls have all the drama. Well, they can't say I didn't try."

Amy walked up to the door of a simple-looking, small brick house and knocked on the door. Dan watched as a woman opened up the door and chatted with Amy for a moment, but he couldn't make out what they were saying.

A moment later, Amy was walking down the steps with little red-cheeked Marty Hunter holding her hand. He walked like a drunken duck, still unsure of how his feet worked. His mess of brown hair covered his light brown eyes, as he tried to move it away with his free hand. Marty looked up at Amy and gave her a goofy smile, his new teeth still too big for his mouth.

As Dan watched, he missed being a little, when everything was simpler and being happy was easy. *When did life get so complicated?*

Dan sighed. "I've got to get going. Y'know, work," he said, as he waved at them and ran off.

He turned around to see Amy and Marty waving, and wondered if life would ever become simple again. He doubted it.

CHAPTER NINETEEN

When in the air, all of Matt's problems seemed to melt away. On the ground, however, they wouldn't leave him alone.

Matt couldn't help but play his conversation with Dan over and over in his head, always thinking of other things he should've said instead. Matt tried to push the thoughts out, but there was always something worse to replace them, like thoughts of Evan.

Matt couldn't shake the thought that maybe Evan's death wasn't an accident. He was ashamed to admit it, but he really hoped it wasn't. If Evan *was* murdered somehow, that meant less guilt for Matt. That meant someone sabotaged the car, and he wasn't responsible for Evan's death. And Evan seemed to think that someone was out to get him, and Matt was sure that as Spark, Evan had a lot of enemies. It made sense. Although that would've meant someone knew Spark's secret identity.

Matt shuttered at the thought. No, Evan was more careful than that. Heck, he didn't even mention his name in any of his journals. But obviously, if the accident wasn't an accident, *someone* must've known. That's assuming, of course, that it was actually possible for someone else to cause the accident.

Matt was so lost in thought he almost walked right past his destination. He caught himself, and walked toward the small white building. Grime was everywhere, and the paint was peeling. Matt looked up at the tattered, faded sign, which read 'Joe's Auto Body Shop – Oil Change Only $20!' Two of the garages were opened, and Matt noticed one of the cars being raised on a hydraulic lift.

He entered through the smudged glass door. Inside were two wooden chairs with tattered seats, a bunch of car magazines that were at least two years old, and an unoccupied counter. Matt reached the counter and rang the bell. When no one came after a minute, he rang it again.

A short bald man in a dirty with a thick mustache and beady little eyes entered from the door behind the counter. He had a grease smudge on his forehead. His name tag read "Lars."

"Yeah?" he asked, in a gruff voice. "Can I help you?" He seemed annoyed to be pulled away from working in the shop.

"Hi, um, I'm Matt Stone. My father's car was in here a little while ago?"

"Oh, yeah, the Stone car," Lars said, wistfully. "Sorry about your... brother, was it?"

"Yeah, my brother, thanks." Matt paused to swallow. "Can I ask you a few questions about the car? Like what condition it was in when it was brought to you?"

"Yeah, it was pretty banged up alright. Real shame." Lars shook his head.

"Was there anything suspicious?" Matt asked.

"Suspicious?" Lars said, raising his eyebrows. "Suspicious like what?"

"I don't know, like if someone cut the brakes or something," Matt said, getting exasperated.

"Whoa, calm down, little man!" Lars said laughing. "I didn't see any cut brake lines or nothing." He paused for a minute, thinking. "Well, we checked the brakes, but we didn't check the power steering fluid. I guess if it was drained that coulda' contributed to the accident." Lars then shook his head. "Nah, probably nothin'. It was a runna' the mill accident, they happen all the time. It's not healthy to look for someone to blame, kid. You just gotta accept this kinda' stuff, y'know?"

Matt nodded as if in understanding. *So it is possible the car was sabotaged*, he thought. The power steering fluid could have been drained. But how could he prove it?

Matt's head began to hurt. Maybe it *was* best just to accept what happened. Chances are it was just that, a freak accident. And if it wasn't an accident, there was no way to know who was responsible anyway. And even if he could figure that all out, Matt had no idea how to deal with such information.

It's not like I could just kill the guy.

Matt began walking home, his head throbbing as he contemplated his next step. He wondered if there even was a mystery here at all. Maybe he was looking for one where it didn't exist.

There was something about wearing the suit. And it wasn't just the sense of strength and power the suit offered, or the freedom of flight. No, it was something else. To be wearing something that Evan wore, Matt felt close to him. He could feel Evan's spirit with him as he took to the sky. Matt wondered what it must've been like, Evan's first time flying. Did he see things the way Matt did right now?

For once, Matt appreciated living in the city. It seemed so peaceful from up above. So serene. So quiet. Floating between the towering skyscrapers, while seven million people scurried about their lives below.

As he flew, weaving through the forest of skyscrapers, Matt looked for any crimes in progress. That's what heroes do, right? He realized he wasn't even sure what to be looking out for. By the time he crawled into bed at three in the morning, Matt felt as though he had wasted his night. Reality and exhaustion hit him at once. As he tried to fall asleep, the same thought played in his head over and over.

He missed Dan.

CHAPTER TWENTY

Alan Swift considered himself to be an honest man, above all else. He was honest with others and honest with himself. And being honest with oneself is the most difficult type of honesty. Most people don't realize just how often they lie to themselves. Many people convince themselves that they have a shot at getting that girl, when if they thought about it honestly for even a minute, they'd realize that they didn't have a chance. Another common lie people tell themselves is they'll start eating healthy tomorrow, when they find themselves saying that line over and over every day. But perhaps the most common lie people tell themselves is that, deep in their heart, they're a good person. Because if they thought for a moment that they weren't, how could they sleep at night? And lying is always easier than trying to change.

Alan didn't always like being so honest. It made him realize truths about himself he'd rather not have to face. But the truth was the truth. Fact. Unavoidable. And the truth was, Alan was a hired gun. True, he was a performer. But more often than not he was working for clients, developing weapons or advising on plans, never letting himself consider what the cost might be to others. And the honest truth was, it had begun to bother him.

Alan paced around the room, kicking stray items that crossed his path across the floor. He had two client meetings today. He glanced up at one of the many screens lining the wall. One of the many rooftop cameras he had lining the city skyline picked up Spark the other day.

He cocked his head. Curious.

Alan was quite familiar with how Spark moved, but here Spark was moving strangely. Perhaps the hero wasn't feeling all that well, Alan reasoned.

There was a knock on the door. It was slow. Methodical. A chill went up his spine as Alan hurried to the door. This was a client he didn't want to keep waiting.

As he opened the door, he found himself face to face with a short, but thin man with sharp features and a shockingly bright head of orange hair. His face was gaunt, and there was a large red burn scarring the lower right corner of his face. His steel-blue eyes were sunken in, glinting dangerously. He casually played with a red lighter as he cocked an eyebrow.

"Are you just going to stand there? Or invite me in?"

"Pyromaniac! Of course, pardon my manners. Come in." As the Pyromaniac walked in, Alan grimaced. "So, you're out?" he said, trying to make conversation.

"Wouldn't be here if I wasn't," the Pyromaniac said as he sat down on the chair, leaning back as his mud-stained boots rested on the table. Chips of dried mud fell onto the table's surface.

Alan winced, but knew better than to stop him. He had to be living if he hoped to ever still perform.

"Bellevue has got to up their security," the Pyromaniac said with a haunting laugh.

Alan laughed nervously. "So, the usual?"

The Pyromaniac shook his head. "Last time my flamethrower ran out of juice too fast. That's how Dragonfly got me thrown into Bellevue in the first place."

"Hm. So you want a flamethrower that'll last longer? Just so you know, it'll be heavier. You might have a difficult time carrying it."

The Pyromaniac chuckled. "I'll take my chances."

"Where are you hitting, by the way?" Alan asked, trying to sound casual.

"I was thinking an apartment building this time," the Pyromaniac said with a smirk.

"Oh." Alan knew he had to think quickly. "Well, there's a few buildings near the Brooklyn Bridge, on the Brooklyn side. You might want to look into that. And there aren't even any cops around between one-thirty and two in the morning."

The Pyromaniac stood up, studying Alan's face. Alan found himself not breathing.

"That's a wonderful idea! Thank you!" the Pyromaniac said enthusiastically.

Alan breathed a sigh of relief. "So I'll text you when the new flamethrower's ready, along with the price."

"Sounds great, friend!" the Pyromaniac said as he walked out the door, winking at Alan before closing it.

Alan slumped down in his chair. That was a close one. He wasn't sure the Pyromaniac would buy it. At least now when he's burning whatever he's burning, he'll be doing it right when and where Spark patrols. Alan felt a weight being lifted off his shoulders.

It's Spark's problem now, he told himself.

There was another knock on the door. This one was quick and irregular. It sounded almost nervous. Alan lifted himself up excitedly. This was a client he was actually looking forward to meeting, if the man was anything like his emails. He leaped to the door and opened it.

The man in the doorway had blond hair and a thin face, which he tried to hide by raising the collar of his trench coat. He was visibly sweating as he looked around nervously.

"You must be Mr. McCoy. Come in!"

"It's Jacob," he said as he grabbed Alan's hand and shook it. It was dripping with sweat.

"Jacob, then," Alan said, wiping his hand on his lab coat. "Come in, please."

Jacob McCoy nodded and walked in. As Alan took a seat, he motioned for Jacob to take the one next to him.

Jacob shook his head. "I-I'd r-rather stand," he said as he shifted around uneasily, eyes glancing around the messy room.

Alan nodded. My, he's a squirrely one, he thought. "So you're idea for a device that produces a localized electromagnetic pulse is intriguing. I've been having a lot of fun working on it. I'm just curious though, what's your big plan. You're a new player, and I must say, I'm intrigued."

"Oh, um, w-well I was thinking I could use it to cut the power to places and rob them, so I w-wouldn't have to worry about alarms a-and stuff," Jacob said nervously. Alan suspected Jacob was *always* nervous.

"That seems rather...ordinary. You have no big supervillain plans?"

"W-well I was th-thinking I'd call myself Blackout, d-dominator of darkness."

Alan stifled a chuckle. This guy was *hilarious*. "Blackout, hm? Not a bad name. I know a guy that could make you a costume."

"I-if it works, I w-won't need one."

"Touché." Alan smiled. Jacob McCoy was sharper than he looked. After a moment, Alan noticed Jacob staring at him, unspeaking. "Yes?"

"Um, th-the localized EMP device?"

"Oh, right!" Alan exclaimed, motioning to a small black device sitting on the table. "Now I have it ready, I think. I still haven't tested it obviously. Too many electronic devices here I'd rather not ruin."

"W-well I s-suppose I'll have to t-test it out myself," Jacob said as he took out of his pocket a rolled-up wad of cash, which was drenched in sweat, and put it on the table.

Alan looked at the sweat and dried mud on the table, then the usual mess around him.

I *really have to clean this place up*, Alan thought.

CHAPTER TWENTY-ONE

"Mr. Stone!"

Matt jerked awake. His blond hair was pressed against his forehead, along with a red pressure mark, with another on his arm to match. Matt wasn't surprised. He had fallen asleep in class again.

"I'm sorry," Matt mumbled, though it sounded less than convincing.

Mr. Winter's eyes narrowed.

"What was the question?" Matt asked. A few students chuckled.

Mr. Winter was visibly annoyed, his face redder than it usually was. "I didn't ask you anything. I just need my class to pay attention!" he yelled. "This isn't kindergarten, and we don't have nap time! Please try to sleep on your own time, not on mine!"

Matt heard more laughing from his classmates. He found it difficult to process what was being said, although that was understandable, considering he'd had just three and a half hours of sleep the night before.

"Sorry." He mumbled sheepishly.

Mr. Winter looked at him intently, as if trying to determine his sincerity, before he continued on with his lecture on late 19th-century political alliances.

Matt sighed and slumped back in his seat. The past few weeks he hadn't been getting much sleep. Not because of the nightmares, not anymore. He had spent the last several weeks flying around the city, looking for crime. Unfortunately, finding crime in New York isn't as easy as movies would lead one to believe. There aren't shootings or robberies on every street corner, and super villain attacks were rare to begin with, only happening every month or so, as far as Matt knew. He felt as though he was failing his brother. Since getting the Spark suit Matt had done nothing but gone on joyrides. He had a name to live up to. Not to mention there was still the circumstances of the accident, or rather, the murder. It just couldn't be that Matt was responsible. Evan's diary seemed to think that his life was in danger. The car *must've* been sabotaged.

The idea had crossed Matt's mind that maybe the car was tampered with by someone trying to get to his mother. It *was* her car, after all. But when he had confronted her a few nights ago, she, rather confusingly, insisted that she didn't have any enemies, and even left her old boss on amicable terms. Matt was able to tell by the look on her face she was worried about him. And in her defense, he *did* sound paranoid. But he knew that *someone* tampered with the car. That was the only explanation. And someone did it specifically to kill Spark.

After history class, Matt headed to his locker, where he found Amy waiting for him. Matt had been avoiding both Dan and Amy the past few weeks, but he should've expected Amy would try something like this sooner or later when he wouldn't return her texts.

"You've been avoiding us," Amy said.

"You should be a detective," Matt responded wryly.

Amy gave him an irritated look. She wasn't amused. "I get you're going through a hard time, and I've been trying to give you your space, but you don't have to become a complete jerk!"

"What am I supposed to do?" Matt retorted angrily. "Be happy all the time? Go over to Dan and say 'I'm sorry?' You don't know—"

He stopped. She was right. Of course she was. He was being a jerk. But swallowing his pride wasn't something Matt could easily do. Amy looked at him quizzically. Matt sighed and began walking away.

"Wait!" Amy called out. Matt gritted his teeth and turned to face her. "First thing, you forgot to actually put your books back in your locker, and second, we can't begin to know what you're going through, we know that. But you've become difficult to be around. We don't want to lose you." Amy's deep brown eyes seemed as though they were about to well up. "You're my best friend."

Amy always seemed to understand. She always seemed to know just the right thing to say. Reluctantly, a smile spread across Matt's face.

"Is that a smile I see? Someone call Eyewitness News!" Amy joked.

"Yeah, yeah, just let Dan know I want to speak with him after school," Matt replied.

Amy smiled as she walked away.

Matt had been waiting outside the school for the past few minutes, waiting for Dan to come out. He mentally ran through how the conversation would go in his head, over and over, each time with a different outcome. Matt spotted Dan's bright yellow sneakers as he walked out of the building, his hair a mess and his button-down shirt tucked in, as usual. Dan greeted Matt with a half wave, and Matt responded in kind. Then Matt froze, suddenly forgetting all his mental preparation.

"Amy said you wanted to meet with me?" Dan said as Matt approached.

Matt became flustered. Why was this so hard? "H-hey, listen I'm sorry about before." Matt mumbled. "I really am. I don't know. I'm just... and my... pride, I guess. Shouldn't have taken this long." As Matt spoke, his voice became clearer. He felt as though a burden was lifting. "I'm really sorry."

"I know. And I'm sorry about not showing up right after Evan, you know, I mean, I was dealing with some stuff, but that's no excuse." Dan said. "And I know I can be a little too sensitive sometimes I need thicker skin. I feel like I wasn't cut out for high school, you know?"

"Hey, if anyone's been too sensitive, it's me." Replied Matt. "Don't worry, we'll make it out of here together." Matt smiled, though Dan could tell it was a fake one. Matt knew Spark probably wouldn't survive long enough for him to make it out of high school. "So are we cool?"

"Yeah, we're cool," Dan said, a smile forming across his face.

As Matt looked at Dan, he realized he couldn't keep this secret to himself. Matt promised himself that he wouldn't end up like Evan—paranoid, and with no friends to trust. He and Dan had been together since second grade. That has to count for something, right? Besides, if there's anyone who knew anything about superheroes, it was Dan, and Matt could use all the help he could get.

"Hey, can I tell you something?" Matt asked seriously.

Dan's grin faded away, thanks to Matt's serious tone. "Sure, what is it?"

"This is important. It's the biggest thing I've ever told anyone. This had to be just between us."

"Matt, you can trust me," Dan said urgently. The feeling of suspense had begun to creep into his voice.

"We're having a memorial for Evan tonight," Matt said. "I'll tell you after."

Dan nodded just as his phone started to buzz. He looked down at it. "That's my alarm! I'm late for my internship!" He exclaimed as he began backing away. "See you later!"

"Yeah, later!" Matt replied as he watched Dan run off.

CHAPTER TWENTY-TWO

It had been a month since Evan's passing. The memorial service was held for him in a mostly white room, rented out from a nearby synagogue. It was a small affair, with the family in attendance, and a few friends and neighbors.

Compared to the lives Evan had effected, thought Matt, this crowd is minuscule. Evan deserved more. Spark deserved more.

Amy and Dan were there, dressed in formal attire. Dan was even wearing a pair of shiny leather dress shoes.

There was some food, a few speeches, and a slideshow was shown, mostly comprised of home videos and sappy music. It was the sort of standard slideshow that was meant to get the audience tearful, while not actually showing any personality of the deceased.

It was while watching the slideshow that it finally sunk in for Matt. For the past three weeks, he had been consumed with Spark. But the realization that this wasn't some grand adventure finally dawned on him. He didn't have a brother anymore. Evan was really gone.

The impact of what had occurred still had not fully hit Matt until that moment. How could it, when his brother had been running on rooftops just a month before? How could it be that now Matt's hero was now six feet below the earth? It seemed impossible, considering the odds Evan had survived before.

Throughout the ceremony, Matt thought with bitter amusement that if this was just what it looked like, it was a death no one could have predicted for Spark. An accident. Now, an early death for superheroes was not unexpected. People like Evan rarely lasted more than a couple of years. Matt realized that he had inadvertently told Evan numerous times that he would likely end up killed by a bullet, or more likely, an elaborate death trap. But no, it was a simple traffic accident. Losing control of the car on an errand. The most recent superhero of New York died at the hands of a concrete divider. Or that's what someone wanted Matt to think. But he knew that couldn't be true. Heroes didn't die like that. It had to be at the hands of some nefarious villain. Evan's death was no mere accident. And Matt would prove that. Somehow.

An uncomfortable thought popped in his head. Would he follow his brother to an early grave? Is *that* Evan's legacy? As Matt closed his eyes, he inhaled. His head began to swim. Despite being surrounded by roses, all he could smell was gunpowder.

The whole thing seemed to last longer than it should have. By the end, Matt was anxious to leave, but he knew he and his family would have to stay long after most people had left.

After the ceremony, Matt came home to find Dan sitting on his stoop, looking at his shoes as he was tapping his feet. As Matt approached, Dan looked up.

Dan opened his mouth. "Hey, so-"

"I need to show it to you." Matt interrupted. "Let's go inside first."

Matt ran up the steps, Dan followed, with a nervous look on his face. He wasn't sure where Matt was going with this. As soon as they were both in Matt's room, he locked the door. Dan looked confused. Matt had never been this secretive before.

"Remember, this is just between us," Matt said as he pulled out the trunk. "People would kill over this. Someone already died because of it."

This was becoming too much for Dan. He was never that patient a person. "Listen, you know you can trust me," he said nervously, sweat beginning to appear on his brow, "But are you sure I want to know?"

Matt grinned. "Oh, I'm sure."

As Matt opened the trunk, Dan froze. His eyes grew wide and his jaw dropped. After what felt like forever, all Dan could bring himself to do was whisper.

"Holy smokes!"

CHAPTER TWENTY-THREE

Dan's shock seemed to have subsided somewhat, and he seemed as excited as a kid in a candy store.

"So how long have you been Spark?"

"A few weeks, though I haven't done much. Evan was *really* Spark. I'm just... I don't know, trying to carry on his legacy, I guess."

"Oh," Dan said, not sure how to react. He flipped through the journals for a few moments. "Have you always known?"

"No. I just found out three weeks ago." Matt responded. "Near as I can tell, he never told anyone."

"Do you think it had anything to do with..." Dan's voice trailed off.

"I think it's a possibility," Matt said carefully. He didn't want to give away how sure he was just yet. He was worried Dan would think he was being paranoid, or just trying to push the blame of Evan's death off himself.

"Hm," Dan responded as he lifted up the Spark suit. "This is so cool!" He said, inspecting it. "Hey, did you know there's bluetooth in the ears?"

"What, really?" Matt hadn't noticed that. Then again, Matt wasn't all that tech savvy.

"Yeah, and check this out!" Dan said, pressing a button on the side of one of the gloves. Matt looked, curiously. He hadn't noticed it before. An electric crackle seemed to come from the glove, as blue sparks danced around the fingers.

"Huh. I guess the Spark name makes some sense now." Matt commented.

"Have you stopped any crimes yet?" Dan asked.

Matt chuckled. "No. It's harder to find than you think."

Dan smiled. "I can help you with that. I've got a police scanner at home. You know, to see if I hear anything close by a superhero might respond to." He looked up wistfully. "I actually saw Dragonfly once."

"So you'd be able to find crime for me to fight?"

"Yeah!" Dan said excitedly. "We can be a team! Like Batman and Oracle!" Noting Matt's confused expression, Dan explained. "Oracle was Batman's computer person."

"Ah." Matt nodded in understanding.

"Hey, we're going to tell Amy, right?" Dan asked, though he obviously already had an answer in mind.

"Not yet. There's no reason to get her involved in this at the moment." Amy was a good girl, and Matt knew what he and Dan were doing was certainly illegal.

Dan nodded reluctantly. "So are you going out patrolling tonight?"

"Nah, it's late already and I'm drained. I think I'm gonna call it a night. Besides, if I fall asleep in history class again, Mr. Winter is gonna flip!"

"Well, we're definitely trying out the bluetooth thing tomorrow. You just keep your phone in your pocket and

I'll be able to tell you where the police scanner says there's trouble."

Matt yawned. "Yeah, tomorrow."

The next day in school marked the first time in weeks that Matt joined Amy and Dan for lunch. He put down his food tray on the white tabletop as he sat down next to Dan. Matt and Dan exchanged knowing glances. Amy grinned.

"So I see you two made up," she said, looking quite pleased with herself. "Gee, I wonder who's responsible for that?"

Matt rolled his eyes. "Oh, don't act so smug, we'd have made up eventually."

"Mhm," Amy said with a deadpan expression. "I'm sure."

Dan was clearly uncomfortable, and desperate to change the conversation to something else. "So did you hear what they're doing at FalconTech?" Dan said earnestly, before adding, "You know, where I intern?" Dan was very proud of that last bit, and he never liked to let an opportunity pass to remind them.

"Hm." Amy thought for a second. "Oh, something about cheap computer tablets, right?"

Matt was confused, understandably. He hadn't heard about any of this. Then again, Matt hadn't really been paying attention to the news these past few weeks. Heck, he rarely paid attention to the news before then either. "Computer tablets?"

"Yeah!" Dan said, unable to hold back his enthusiasm. "See, FalconTech has been working on these new tablets that they're manufacturing, and they're gonna run on a new operating system they've developed. It's supposed to blow the iPad out of the water. I'm actually working on marketing, via social media." He looked around, hoping to find his friends impressed, but was met with blank expressions. Noting the lack of response, he continued. "So anyway, they're doing this big marketing stunt where they're gonna give away tens of thousands of tablets to students throughout the city, preloaded with textbooks, educational videos, the works."

Now Matt and Amy were legitimately impressed and excited.

"So you mean we're going to get free high-end tablets?!" Amy exclaimed.

Dan grinned. "Yep! And I'm working on the social network marketing!"

Noting that he was repeating that last part in an effort to impress them, Matt and Amy oohed and ahhed appropriately.

CHAPTER TWENTY-FOUR

It was a clear night. Matt was standing on the roof on Brooklyn Marriott, overlooking the Manhattan skyline across the river. The lights glittered on the water. He looked up at the sky, wishing the city lights didn't drown out the stars.

Matt, clad in the Spark suit, placed his phone, already ringing, in his pocket. Dan picked up.

"Matt?"

"It works. Cool!" Matt responded. "Got anything for me?"

"You really need to develop a patrol route, you know," Dan replied.

"Hey, cut me some slack, I'm still new at this."

Matt jumped off the building and clicked his feet together, enjoying the moment of weightlessness before the flight kicked in. Matt glided above the East River, as he flew toward Manhattan.

"Wait, we got something," Dan said excitedly. "There's a building on Fulton Street where the silent alarm just went off. It could be nothing, but you should check it out."

Matt was pretty close anyway. "Got it. I'll be there in a few minutes."

When Matt reached the address, he landed on a nearby building and looked around. As he looked down at the people walking below, he marveled at how rarely people ever looked up. As Matt looked around, he noticed a man, clad in black, with a black ski mask and backpack, standing on the building across, staring at him.

When he realized Spark noticed him, he ran toward Spark. Matt hesitated, unsure of what to do. The man clad in black was on a building across the street. There wasn't anywhere for the guy to run.

Then, Matt watched in amazement as the man jumped onto a flagpole sticking out of the brick wall of the building, ran across it effortlessly, and jumped, landing less than a dozen feet away from Spark.

Matt was in awe. He had never seen anything like that in real life before.

"What, you don't recognize me?" The man in black asked. "It's probably the black suit. I didn't think my usual outfit would work for a nighttime burglary."

Matt just stared at him. Should he know this guy? "I'm confused."

"Yes, well I suppose that makes sense. How many people heard of daytime burglaries?" the man said jokingly. "It's me, the Acrobat!"

"The Acrobat?"

"Holy smokes!" Dan said. "The Acrobat! I know him! I've seen footage of him! Holy smokes!" He paused. "Just so you know, Matt, he's never been caught."

"Why would you tell me that? What chance do I have?!"

The Acrobat cocked his head to the side. "Are you talking to someone?"

Matt turned toward him and got into his best heroic pose. "Ah, yes, the Acrobat. Well, Acro, I hope you made friends with lions in the circus, because you're about to join them in a cage!"

Dan laughed in Matt's ear. "Dude, what're you doing? That sounded like a horrible sixties comic book or something."

The Acrobat sounded like he was trying to hold in a chuckle. "Seriously? That was pretty forced."

"I'm new at this!" Matt said defensively.

"At heroic banter? That's apparent. And since when did you make jokes?"

Matt's heart raced. *Well, it's now or never.* He activated the electric charge in his right glove and rushed at the Acrobat, who easily dodged to the left and ran across the edge of the building. Matt breathed heavily.

Man, he's fast.

"C'mon, is that all you got?" The Acrobat taunted. "Go for the 'juggler!'" He snickered at his own awful pun.

Dan, back at his mother's place, had trouble following what was happening. "Matt, what's going on?"

Matt braced himself as the Acrobat ran at him. This time Matt got both his hands ready, looking at them as they crackled with electricity. The Acrobat simply leaped over Matt and kicked his back as he landed. Matt stumbled forward.

"He's too fast!" Matt said to Dan, as he tried to catch his breath.

This was exhilarating. Frustrating, sure, but Matt had never felt as alive as he did now.

He turned to the Acrobat. "Hey, shouldn't your name be the Gymnast or something?"

The Acrobat didn't answer the question as he stood at the other edge of the building, balancing on one foot. "Come on," he taunted. "Are we going to fight, or are you just going to *clown* around? I promise this isn't a *trap-ese!*"

Matt rolled his eyes. With his sense of humor, the man *had* to be a dad. He stared at the Acrobat, analyzing him. Matt's eyes narrowed. The Acrobat was about twenty feet away; Matt was sure he could get him this time.

"Y'know, your puns are the *real* crime!" Matt yelled as he ran and jumped toward the Acrobat.

He clicked his feet together, suddenly flying toward the Acrobat at breakneck speed. As the adrenaline pumped through Matt's body, it seemed as if time itself slowed down. Despite the Acrobat wearing a ski mask, Matt could swear he saw him smile as he fell backwards, off the edge of the building. Matt's hands grabbed the empty air where the Acrobat had just been a split second before. *Just missed him*, he thought, gritting his teeth.

As Matt turned around in midair and looked down, he knew it was too late. He expected to see the black-clad body splattered over the sidewalk, but there was no trace of a body anywhere.

The Acrobat had gotten away.

"He's gone!" Matt yelled in frustration.

"What do you mean he's gone!?!" Dan exclaimed.

"He's just gone! Poof! Gone!"

"Yeah, well he was a pretty well-known thief, and this was our first go, don't be so hard on yourself," Dan replied, trying to comfort Matt.

Matt grunted.

"Hey, there's a fire in an apartment building in the DUMBO neighborhood, you know, right near the bridge." Dan said. "Want to check it out?"

"Sure, the night's still young." Matt said, as he headed toward the Manhattan Bridge.

CHAPTER TWENTY-FIVE

Matt could see the fire from across the water. Dark pillars of smoke had risen high in the sky, blacking out an already dark sky. As he got closer, he could see flashing red lights. There were several fire trucks and dozens of firefighters in yellow fireproof clothing milling around, trying to keep the crowd that had gathered away from the building.

Matt could make out some people still in pajamas and slippers. A little girl was clutching her stuffed animal, her face covered in soot. He looked back at the building. Flames leapt from the windows, dancing hypnotically.

Matt landed a good dozen feet away, but could still feel the intense heat. He began sweating. The leathery material of the suit felt pasted to his skin.

"What's going on?" he called to one of the firefighters.

A uniformed grey-haired man walked over. "Fire," he said simply, with a distinct Brooklyn accent.

Gee, thanks. As if I couldn't see that, Matt thought, rolling his eyes.

"Is there anyone still inside?" he asked through gritted teeth.

The man nodded. "Yeah, a family of three, we think, on the fourth floor. It's too dangerous to go in at the moment though," he replied. The firefighter looked away. "I doubt they're still alive," he added, sadly.

Matt looked at the building, now engulfed in flames. This was it. His chance to be a hero. Just like Evan.

He darted toward the building. The firefighter yelled in protest, but the sound of his voice quickly faded as Matt got close to the crackling blaze. He scanned the windows. All the fourth floor windows were engulfed in fire. He'd have to take the stairs.

Matt ran through the open door. It was hard to see. The power had been cut. He switched to night vision and continued down the hall. He was sweltering in the suit and his hair was damp with sweat. Matt saw a door leading to a stairwell at the end of the hall and ran toward it. He placed his hand on the metal knob to open the door and immediately recoiled. It was burning hot.

Matt was breathing heavily now. No, he had to do this. For that family. For Evan.

He grabbed the doorknob and twisted it, pushing the door open. He could run his hand under cold water later.

Matt raced up the stairs, his feet blurred as they touched only every other step, until he reached the door with a "4" clearly marked. This was it. He kicked the door open.

A blast of heat hit him as an inferno of fire burst forth. Matt was pushed backwards, hitting the far wall. Black smoke quickly filled the room. Matt began coughing uncontrollably. He covered his mouth and gritted his teeth, running into the flames before him. Matt's vision began to blur. He could barely see a foot in front of him. Matt remembered that heat and smoke rises, so he crouched down and began crawling. The visibility was somewhat better.

The heat was unbearable. Matt grimaced. He could smell burning flesh. It took Matt a moment to realize he was smelling himself. He tried calling out, but he only gagged, coughing some more.

Surrounded by the heat, flames, and smoke, in the heart of a fiery inferno, Matt realized he was too late. He wasn't going to be able to save that family. No one could survive this.

His heart pounded as he realized had to get out of there. Matt turned around to find the door where he came from, but couldn't make anything. The smoke had engulfed the room. A large rectangular beam, consumed in fire fell, landing inches away from him.

Matt ran down the hall blindly. There had to be some way out. He tripped, catching himself with his hands as he fell. They were throbbing. His breathing was labored. He looked around desperately, but he might as well have been blindfolded.

No, Matt thought. Not now. Not so soon after Evan.

He lifted himself up, slowly getting to his feet. He could feel his skin start to blister. He ran. Everything became a blur of black and orange. He bumped into something with his knee.

Ignore the pain. Keep going.

Black and orange swirled around him. Suddenly glass shattered around him. He could feel air whooshed past his face. Sweet, wonderful, crisp air.

He was suddenly aware the ground was rushing up to meet him. Matt clicked his feet together just before hitting the ground, taking to the sky. As the adrenalin began to wear off, he became aware of the pain. He groaned.

Dan's voice suddenly exploded in his ear. "Matt! Are you there?"

"What? Yeah." He coughed again. "Just barely. Where were you before?"

"I couldn't hear anything. I think there might've been interference or something."

"I failed, Dan. I didn't save anyone. I'm a sucky superhero."

"You got there too late. There's nothing you could've done."

Matt grunted. "I'm going home. Need to clean myself up." He coughed again. "I'll see you tomorrow."

"Okay. Take care, man." Matt heard a click. Dan had hung up.

Matt coughed yet again. He hoped it wasn't permanent. His hair and the Spark suit was covered in ash and soot. He needed a shower.

As he flew home, he wondered if he'd ever be worthy to be Evan's replacement. He sure didn't have a high opinion of himself at the moment.

By the time he got home, he collapsed into bed. In his past seventeen years on this earth, he had never been so exhausted. That night, Matt dreamed a dreamless sleep.

CHAPTER TWENTY-SIX

Alan started his day as he usually did. A cup of hot cocoa while reading the newspaper. Alan sat down with his steaming mug, and took a sip as he turned on the tablet, where the newspaper should've already been loaded. The screen lit up. The mug slipped from his hand. It wasn't a long drop, and it landed right side up, but hot cocoa splashed everywhere. Alan didn't seem to notice. He stared at his tablet in disbelief.

No, this couldn't be right, he thought. It just couldn't. The headline stared back, mocking him.

TRAGIC ARSON IN DUMBO CLAIMS THREE LIVES

A fire broke out last night at a residential building near the Brooklyn Bridge. The fire led to the tragic death of three people, including a child. The fire is suspected to be an arson attack, with Alexander Jason, more commonly known as the 'Pyromaniac' the prime suspect. Jason had recently escaped from Bellevue Hospital, where he was being treated for... Click here to read the full story.

Alan felt sick. Something churned in his stomach. He could feel something pressing down on this chest making it difficult to breathe. Alan began rubbing his forehead. It was already moist with sweat.

Is this what guilt feels like?

A family was dead because of him. A child was no longer breathing because of something he had done.

No, that's not true. It was the Pyromaniac. Why should Alan feel guilty? All he did was build the flamethrower.

This wasn't my fault, Alan told himself. I even directed him to the perfect time and place to get caught by Spark.

Spark.

It was all Spark's fault. Of course it was. He was supposed to be there. He should've been there.

So why wasn't he?

Alan grabbed the nearest laptop, opened it, and began typing frantically, trying to pull up a video of last night's events. He was sure that he had a camera somewhere in the vicinity that picked up something.

He found and pulled up a video that was time-stamped and had a decent view of the building. He watched as the Pyromaniac entered the building, a flamethrower of Alan's design strapped to his back. Alan played the video in fast forward. He watched as the Pyromaniac ran out of the building just as smoke started billowing from the windows.

Where was Spark?

As the minutes passed, the smoke got darker. Flames began to leap from the windows.

There was still no sign of Spark.

This is his patrol route! How could he have been late?

Finally, Spark showed up, landing in front of the building and standing around like an idiot before eventually flying in.

Alan drew his mouth to a line. Something was very off.

He replayed the footage again, studying it carefully. The way Spark was moving was strange. Unfamiliar. Suddenly it hit him.

The performers were switched out on me, he thought as he felt a jolt of adrenaline pump through his body. Someone else is playing Spark's role!

Alan gritted his teeth. How could he have not realized it earlier? And for that matter, how long had this imposter been around? Alan's heart began beating rapidly. Solving mysteries was not unlike inventing. All one has to do is identify the issue, gather the necessary information, and solve it.

Alan clicked an icon, opening a folder containing hundreds of video files with thousands of hours of footage, stretching back through the last month.

This was going to take a while.

CHAPTER TWENTY-SEVEN

It was abnormally hot for so early in the spring, and it was certainly abnormally hot for so early in the morning. The black asphalt had waves of heat rising above it, and to the touch felt hot enough to fry an egg or two. Dan and Matt were standing out in front of the school.

Dan wished the earth rotated in the opposite direction that day, which would have allowed the two of them to stay cool in the shade of the red-bricked building. Instead, they were baking under the heat.

Matt was trying not to think about the fire from the night before, something the ever-present heat made difficult. He wondered if any superheroes actually wore their costumes under their clothes, or if that was exclusive to the realm of comic books and movies. He couldn't understand how anyone could wear anything extra in weather like this. The bright sun blinded Matt. Squinting, he cupped a hand above his brow, which had already begun to collect sweat.

"So I was thinking I should probably sign up for karate or something. I have no clue how to fight. What was I thinking?" Matt seemed frustrated.

Dan looked around the school yard to make sure no one was listening. Class didn't start for another twenty minutes, so the school was still fairly deserted. Often, most people just barely made it on time.

"Listen do you think Evan was good starting out? These things take practice and experience. You did fine."

Matt laughed. "You didn't see me. It was awful. I mean, Acrobat was-"

"Hi, Amy!" Dan interrupted, waving.

Matt turned around to see Amy walking toward them, her face shining with perspiration and her brown hair in a ponytail. She smiled as she saw them. Matt couldn't help but notice pit stains had already begun to form beneath her arms upon her light blue shirt. He averted his eyes and made a mental note to avoid looking there.

"Hey, guys! Do anything interesting last night?"

"Nah," Matt lied. "Just homework."

Dan found it harder to lie than Matt, and he didn't like being dishonest to Amy. After all, during his fight with Matt, she was his only friend.

"Well I saw Arthur Falcon yesterday," Dan said honestly. "You know, the founder of FalconTech?"

"Cool," Amy said somewhat dismissively, obviously having only asked the question so she could answer it herself. "So I finally saw The Notebook last night!"

"The Notebook?!" Matt scoffed.

"Eh, I thought it was ok for a chick flick." Dan countered.

"It's horrible. The guy is a total stalker!" Matt replied, practically yelling.

"Hey," said Amy. "I thought it was romantic!"

"Of course *you* did," Matt said. Dan laughed.

"What does *that* mean?!" Amy exclaimed defensively.

"It was abusive!" Matt argued. "He threatened to kill himself if she didn't date him. How is that okay?!"

"C'mon, he wasn't really gonna kill himself!" Dan argued. "He was just trying for the classic grand romantic gesture!"

"She lied to and cheated on that totally awesome fiancé of hers!" Matt exclaimed, aware he was getting a little too invested in the argument.

"So she was flawed, sure," Amy said. "So was he. But being flawed doesn't mean they're bad people. It simply means they're flawed. Like all of us. It still makes for a beautiful story."

Dan and Matt were silent for a moment.

"Wow, got you guys speechless," Amy laughed. "Someone should be recording this moment for posterity!"

Matt smiled. It felt like old times again, Matt thought. The Three Musketeers. Dan grinned as well, but it was fake. Plastic. There was an invisible barrier separating him and Matt from Amy. He and Matt shared a secret. A secret Dan felt she should know.

The bell rang.

CHAPTER TWENTY-EIGHT

Matt looked out of his window. The sky seemed unusually clear. It was a full moon tonight, or very close to one. He could even make out a few stars, which was something of a rarity in the city.

Matt put on the mask, and careful not to make any noise, he opened his window and climbed out onto the ledge.

"We really should tell her." Dan's voice came out of Matt's earpiece.

"It's better if she doesn't know, Dan," Matt said, frustrated, as he jumped off the ledge and took to the air.

Matt wondered if there was going to be any action tonight. It had been a week since the fire, and all he'd done since then was help a kitten out of a tree. He was hungry for more action. He still hadn't made a difference since taking the Spark mantle, and he felt he owed it to Evan. It's been over a month and he hadn't stopped a single crime or saved a single person.

I'm a failure, he thought. But I can't let Evan down.

"Why? Why can't we tell her?" Dan said, still not letting the Amy issue go. "Because being a vigilante is illegal? Listen, if you're caught, she has just as much of a chance of getting in trouble as I do. They'll assume your best friends were involved. They always do."

"It's my secret to tell, and we're not telling her, okay?"

Matt was angry. Even flying couldn't lighten his mood. He wondered if perhaps Dan's insistence on telling Amy was bothering him so much because maybe Dan was right.

"Whatever," Dan grumbled. "Oh, and looks like we've got some trouble right here in Brooklyn. All the power suddenly went out in the Kings Plaza Mall."

"Isn't the mall closed now?" Matt asked, altering his course toward Flatbush Avenue.

"Well yeah," Dan replied, "But that's no reason for the power to go out. I'm thinking burglary."

"Of course you are. It could be a blackout, you know. Or a blown fuse."

"Yeah, but if it was a blackout, it wouldn't be the only building affected," Dan explained. "And there's no reason for the fuse to just blow like that."

"Yeah, yeah, I hear you," Matt said as the mall appeared up ahead, its lights out, like a dark grey monolith among bright streetlights.

Matt was in the process of landing on the building when suddenly the rockets in his boots gave out, causing him to fall the last three feet.

"Ouch." He stumbled as he tried to get up. "Dan, what the heck happened? It's like my suit just gave out."

Silence.

This didn't make sense. It couldn't be happening. It just couldn't. Matt remembered he had charged the suit before he left.

He frantically tried to click his feet together and activate the gloves' electric jolts, but to no avail. His breathing increased rapidly. Panic set in as Matt pulled out his phone. The screen was blank. He touched the side buttons, but nothing happened. The phone was off.

That's strange. It had been on just seconds before.

Matt held down the side button as he tried to turn it on.

Nothing. The screen remained pitch black.

Anxiety kicked in as Matt looked around the empty rooftop.

He was all alone.

CHAPTER TWENTY-NINE

Matt tried to control his breathing, attempting to fight off the feelings of dread and panic. He closed his eyes for a few seconds, trying to calm down. He remembered the weight of Evan's legacy rested on his shoulders.

I can do this, Matt thought. I have to. For Evan. For his legacy.

He opened his eyes and saw a door not twenty feet away. It must lead down from the roof, he thought as he walked toward it. Matt reached for the door, and it easily swung open. Unlocked. Matt breathed a sigh of relief.

He reached for the light switch.

Nothing.

Of course, Matt thought, mocking himself. Because that would just be too convenient, wouldn't it?

He briefly had a moment of excitement, recalling the suit had night vision, before remembering that the suit wasn't working. As he headed down the steps, Matt reached into his pocket, pulling out his small flashlight. He clicked it, not sure what exactly he expected to happen. Nothing. Again.

He clenched his free hand into a fist in anger. Why would the flashlight work anyway, when nothing else does?

Matt, frustrated, threw the flashlight to the floor where it clattered, the sound echoing down the dark empty staircase.

Reaching out, Matt began to feel his way down the stairs. He found himself enveloped in darkness, his hands pressed against the wall as he descended the narrow staircase. The paint felt old, likely peeling. A dank, moldy smell reached Matt's nostrils, causing a wave of nausea to pass over him.

He silently continued down, the only sounds heard were his own breathing and the muffled thumps of his feet as they met each step. Every so often, he'd hit a wall, and turn to the left to descend another flight.

There was a loud squeak as something ran past Matt's leg. He jumped, then grabbed his mouth to keep himself from making any noise. Matt paused to calm his nerves as he breathed heavily. He then continued to trek downward, deeper into the darkness below.

Matt reached another wall. As he turned, something small and round hit his right side. A doorknob.

Finally.

Matt opened the door, hoping the see something on the other side. Being swallowed by the dark empty blackness in a narrow stairway for the past ten minutes was beginning to make him feel claustrophobic. The door led out to the main walkway on the third floor of the mall.

He looked around, surprised that he could make out anything. It wasn't pitch black, like the staircase. There was a red flickering glow coming out of the storefront on the other end of the mall. Matt raced toward it, not sure of what he expected to find. As he got closer he realized it was a jewelry store, and the glass door had been shattered.

As Matt peered inside, he saw a lit red flare resting atop a display case. A thin, gaunt man, with brown or blond hair, it was hard to tell in the red light, was kneeling beside it. The man, cloaked entirely in black, was packing jewelry into his backpack, taking his time to admire the sparkling objects as he did so. There were bags under his eyes, and his chin was coated in stubble, as though he hadn't shaved in a few days. As he looked up, his eyes grew wide. The surprise of seeing someone else there was apparent on his face.

"W-Who are you?" he asked nervously. "N-No one w-w-was supposed to be here!"

"What did you do?" Matt asked. "I mean, aside from the obvious." He motioned to the empty display cases and the backpack.

The man stood up, backpack swinging over his shoulder, and puffed out his chest. "P-pretty cool, right?" It was obvious to Matt this guy was pretty new at this. "I'm Blackout! D-dominator of darkness!" He put his hands on his hips for dramatic effect, and gave a sheepish grin. "H-hey, Y-you're Spark, aren't you? The superhero?"

"You put a lot of work into that, didn't you?" Matt said, ignoring the question.

"W-well, it was either 'dominator' or 'director.' What do you think? Is the alliteration too much?"

Matt ignored that question too. "What did you do to the power?"

The odd man stared blankly at Matt, as though he didn't understand the question. Finally, nodded as if the realization had just dawned upon him. "O-oh, y-yes, that. W-well I have this little device, see?"

Blackout held out a small rectangular black box, about the size of a voice recorder. "When I press the button, it sends out a localized EMP, uh, an eh-electro-magnetic p-pulse that fries all the nearby electronic circuits," he said proudly. "N-Now I don't h-have to worry about alarms. P-pretty cool, eh?"

Well, that explains why the suit and cell phone stopped working, Matt thought. And it *was* pretty cool, although he wouldn't admit it to Blackout.

Matt took a step toward him and suddenly remembered that he didn't really know how to fight. Heck, without the suit working, he didn't know if he could even stop the guy.

"Well, it's over!" Matt said, in his most authoritative voice, hoping to avoid a physical confrontation. It was hard to seem imposing when he was only five-foot-five, but Matt tried his best anyway. "Time you turn yourself in." Matt didn't think that would work, but Blackout didn't look like much of a fighter.

Blackout paused for a second. "Well, alright."

Matt was surprised and relieved.

Blackout then darted right past Matt, out the door. Matt was stunned for a moment.

"Of course he'd lie! He's a criminal!" Matt mumbled to himself as he grabbed the flare and began to chase Blackout through the empty mall, now bathed in red light.

Matt stopped for a moment, listening for any sound. He heard the patter of feet, and turned to see Blackout running down the now-frozen escalator. Matt knew he could never reach him in time. Thinking quickly, he threw the flare, hoping it would hit its mark.

As the flare collided with Blackout's arm, he tripped. A yell escaped his mouth, as he began tumbling down the rest of the steps. Matt reached the escalator to find Blackout stumbling away on the floor below. Matt knew at this point pursuit was useless. Blackout was mere feet away from the exit, and once outside would be able to blend in with the crowd.

Matt sighed as he slowly descended the escalator. He felt worn out and tired, but more than anything he felt like a failure. He'd had the suit for weeks, but didn't manage to stop a single crime.

Some hero he turned out to be.

As Matt reached the bottom of the escalator, he thought about just hanging up the suit. After all, it looked like he was ruining Evan's legacy more than anything. He sighed again.

As Matt knelt down to pick up the flare, he noticed something next to it. A little black box.

The EMP device!

Matt picked it up and looked it over. There was a little switch on the side. He turned the device off, expecting the lights to suddenly go back on. Nothing happened. Then Matt remembered that electromagnetic pulses fried electronics, often ruining the internal circuitry permanently.

He slipped the device in his pocket and began making his way toward the exit, wondering how he was going to get home without the suit operational and no change to take a bus. The thought most prevalent in Matt's head was that he made a huge mistake. He never should've become Spark. He wasn't like Evan. The whole endeavor had been a complete failure thus far.

As he neared the exit, there was a bright flash. Matt nearly fell over in surprise. Everything had suddenly turned green! He hesitated for a second as he processed it. Night vision! Of course!

Matt quickly tested the gloves and watched in glee as the blue sparks danced around in the palms of his hands. He pulled out his phone. Dan would be worried about him. He tried to turn it on, but was unsuccessful. Matt wasn't sure how the suit managed to survive the EMP and still remain operational, but he wasn't complaining. He dashed out the door and took to the air.

As he neared his house, he noticed someone sitting on the stoop, waiting. Matt landed in the side yard, hoping the neighbors didn't see.

"Dan? Is that you?" he whispered.

Dan rushed to Matt. "What the heck was that? You just cut out in middle of a conversation? You had me worried sick! I maybe thought you died or something!" Dan was hyperventilating. It looked like he was having an anxiety attack.

"My phone's dead." Matt said, holding up his cell. "Look, I'm fine, alright? How'd you sneak out anyway?"

"When your parents are getting a divorce, you can get away with pretty much anything," Dan said, the bitterness apparent in his voice.

"Ah," Matt said, feeling uncomfortable and unsure of how to respond. He sighed. "Look, I don't feel comfortable talking outside my house dressed like this, I had a crazy night, and its two-freakin'-thirty in the morning. Can I just fill you in on what happened tomorrow?"

Dan looked at Matt, as though he was judging him on the veracity of his words. "Alright," Dan finally said with a sigh, followed by a yawn. "See you tomorrow."

CHAPTER THIRTY

Dan was eager to get to school the next day. Although to be fair, Dan was usually eager to get to school. His home was not a place he liked being around anymore. But today he couldn't wait to get there more so than usual.

Dan sent Matt a couple of texts that morning, but had received no reply. He wanted to hear Matt explain himself. Dan was angry at first, thinking last night Matt should've borrowed someone's phone to let him know he was okay, or maybe call him from a payphone, before realizing that working payphones were practically nonexistent now, and how ridicules it would've been outside of Times Square or a comic book convention for someone dressed as a superhero to ask a stranger on the street to borrow a cell phone.

As he raced to school, Dan couldn't help but think that Matt wasn't making the best choices, and the thought that perhaps *he* would've been a better superhero crossed his mind. Dan knew he couldn't entirely trust his own judgment though, and was sure part of him was jealous of Matt. Dan would never tell him that, of course.

Upon reaching the courtyard of the school, Dan paused to catch his breath. He always enjoyed his morning runs to school, though admittedly preferred colder weather to the current heatwave. He looked down at his sneakers, which had started to fray. A heavy sigh escaped Dan's mouth. He really liked those sneakers, but he'd have to get new ones soon. Dan hated change, but that seemed to be all his life was lately.

There was a tap on his shoulder. He turned, expecting it to be Matt. Much to Dan's surprise, it was Amy, all smiles as usual. He tried to hide the disappointment on his face, knowing that now he'd have to wait for another opportunity to speak to Matt alone, because it sure wasn't happening this morning.

"Hey, Amy!" He said, smiling in an attempt to hide his frustration.

"Guess what came in the mail yesterday?" Amy asked, obviously intending to answer the question herself. Dan opened his mouth to answer when Amy, who obviously couldn't hold in her excitement any longer, just blurted it out. "My driver's license!" she exclaimed gleefully.

"Wow, that's amazing!" Dan said with the most enthusiastic voice he could muster. They talked for a bit about cars and driving, and of course Brooklyn's obvious lack of parking spaces until the bell rang.

Dan wished he could talk to her about Spark. It was killing him to keep this from her. As they headed inside for class, Dan wondered where Matt was. Probably still sleeping, he reasoned. His mood worsened.

As Dan was headed toward the cafeteria during the lunch period, he felt someone grab him and pull him aside. He turned angrily to find Matt's apologetic face.

"Where were you this morning!? I texted you!" Dan hissed.

"I overslept. I'm really sorry. And my cell phone is dead. Like *dead* dead. It won't start up or charge or anything." Matt held up his phone, the screen blank.

"What happened?" Dan asked, losing patience. "Did you drop it last night or something?"

"No, um, it's kinda a long story," Matt said sheepishly. "There was this guy last night, called himself Blackout. He had some kinda EMP device that shorted out all the electricity in the area, including my phone and the suit. Also, he kicked my butt."

"That doesn't make any sense. You flew home last night. I saw you. The circuitry of the suit should've been destroyed, like the phone, if it was an EMP."

"It just rebooted." Matt shrugged. "I don't know anything about science."

"Hm. That's very curious," Dan said, rubbing his imaginary beard. "Maybe your suit is protected from an electromagnetic pulse, and just shuts down temporarily to protect itself. Or maybe it wasn't an electromagnetic pulse at all. Let me see your phone."

Matt handed it to him.

As he studied the phone, Dan said, "I'll take a look at this later today. Maybe it can be fixed. We'll trade back tomorrow."

"Trade?" Matt said, confused.

"Here's mine," Dan said as he handed his phone to Matt. "You'll need it more than I do."

"Wow, thanks!"

"But," Dan said, as Matt's heart sank. There was always a catch. "But you tell Amy." Dan looked at Matt sternly.

"No," Matt said quickly.

Dan was upset. "Look, I get not telling your folks, because yeah, they'd never let you be Spark. They've already lost one kid, they'd never risk losing a second one. But Amy? She's our friend! Your friend! You know we can trust her! And this whole cliché 'don't want to put someone in danger' excuse? News flash, Amy's *already* in danger. She's close to you. Heck, most folks think she's your girlfriend! At least if she knew your secret she'd be aware of the danger she's in!"

Matt was shocked. "People think Amy's my girlfriend?"

Dan viewed Matt with a look of pure frustration. That was *not* what he was supposed to take out of it.

"Alright! Fine. I guess you make sense," Matt said, begrudgingly. "I'll tell her tonight."

"Finally!" Dan exclaimed, with a look of relief on his face.

The two friends entered the cafeteria. As Matt and Dan sat next to Amy, Dan smiled. The invisible barrier in his mind was already fading away.

"Hey, Amy," Matt said nervously.

Amy noticed his expression. "Is everything okay?" she asked, concerned.

"Oh, yeah, fine," Matt replied, as unconvincing as ever. "Hey, can you drop by my place later? I have something important to tell you."

His eyes darted to Dan, as if seeking approval. Dan smiled in return and gave a slight nod.

"Oh, sure," Amy said nonchalantly, pretending not to notice the look Matt and Dan exchanged.

CHAPTER THIRTY-ONE

Night had begun to fall. The sky looked like a battle between orange and pink, each fighting each other for the last few moments of daylight left. A partial moon was already visible, as if hanging from an invisible string in the not-yet-dark sky.

Amy Hunter's heart was pounding. It felt to her like it was beating a million miles a minute. This was it, she thought, as she turned the corner onto Matt's block. She had expected this for a while. All the signs were there, and it was only a matter of time before Matt confided in her. Talking with Dan in hushed tones, the knowing glances, and now this, asking to speak to her privately. It was obvious, Amy thought. Matt had a crush on her, and he was finally going to ask her out.

She wasn't sure how she should react. Yes, she liked Matt, but she never thought of him in a romantic way. Then again, there's no reason she couldn't. He was a sweet, nice guy, and Amy knew she liked spending time with him. And yeah, he was a little shorter than she was looking for in a guy, but so what? He's still pretty adorable, she thought. Not to mention rejecting him would probably ruin their friendship permanently.

Although, on the other hand, a failed romantic relationship would also ruin their friendship permanently.

She approached the house and knocked on the door. She felt as though there was a swarm of hummingbirds fluttering around in her stomach.

Some things are worth the risk, she thought. Besides, if I don't do this, I'll always have the 'what if' question in the back of my mind.

Amy knew she couldn't live like that. Fine, it was settled then. When Matt asks her out tonight, she'll accept.

Matt opened the door. "Hey," he said nervously. "C'mon up to my room."

Amy couldn't help but grin. This was it.

When they got to his room, Amy noticed it had been cleaned up since she had been there last. You could actually make out the floor, and there was no half-eaten food lying about. Even the books were neatly lined up on the shelf. Matt sat down on the bed, and patted the spot next to him, motioning for Amy to sit there. As she sat, she noticed Matt's knees were quivering a little.

Aw, she thought, he's nervous.

"Listen, Amy, there's something I'm going to tell you right now. It's probably the most important thing I'll ever tell you." Matt's voice started shakily, but grew more confident as he spoke. "This has to stay a secret though. No one can know about this. I mean it. No one. Heck, if my parents knew, they'd never let me leave the house."

It took a moment for the words to register before it dawned on her what Matt was trying to say.

Well of course he is, Amy thought as her heart sank. All the good guys are.

"Listen," she began, determined to be the best friend she could possibly be. "You know you can trust me. And I'm really glad you feel close enough to tell me." She looked at him intensely. "Just know I support you no matter what." She paused before adding, "And Dan's a really sweet guy. I'm really happy for you two."

"Wait, what!?!" Matt exclaimed, genuinely confused. He mumbled to himself for a moment, repeating bits of the conversation, going through it in his mind. "Oh, wow! No, Amy, I'm not, I mean I get how you could've thought that, but I'm-"

Amy interrupted. "So what is it then?!" she said, irritated and more confused than ever.

Matt hopped off the bed and ran to the door, ensuring it was locked. "Lift up your feet, please," he asked.

Amy complied with his request. Matt pulled the trunk out from under his bed, turned it to face Amy. This was it, he thought. He opened the trunk. Whatever Amy had prepared for, this was not it. Matt studied her face. Her reaction was more subdued than Dan's. Amy just raised her eyebrows somewhat, as she processed what she was seeing, and what it meant. She picked up the Spark suit, examining it, running her fingers across the blue highlights.

"You're Spark? You're a superhero?" Amy asked in disbelief.

"Well, I'm trying," Matt said. "It was Evan's."

Amy studied the suit intensely, occasionally glancing back at Matt, still trying to process everything. After what seemed like an eternity, she finally spoke.

"Can you fly?" she asked.

"Yeah," Matt replied. "Why?"

"What's it like?"

"Oh," Matt said excitedly. "It's like the most amazing thing ever. It's like pure unadulterated freedom. It's just incredible. I-I don't know how else to describe it."

"Then don't," Amy said, throwing the suit at him. It made a sound like a wet cloth as it hit Matt's chest. "Take me."

Clad in the Spark suit, standing on his roof, Matt looked at Amy, unsure. She was putting on an old pair of swimming goggles Matt found, to protect her eyes. The night air was crisp and cool, a pleasant break from the intense heat of the recent weather. There was a breeze that ruffled Matt's blond hair as it passed by. Matt was nervous about flying while holding another person. He wasn't sure if the suit could take it. He took a deep breath.

"Okay, let's do this," Matt said.

Amy held onto him as he picked her up. The thought crossed Matt's mind that if not for the suit's enhanced strength, he probably wouldn't be able to hold her for long. Even with the enhanced strength, he worried his arms would tire.

"Here goes nothing."

Matt jumped, clicking his feet together. His heart was racing. He closed his eyes. A rush of air hit his face.

"Whooohooo!" Amy shrieked.

Matt opened his eyes. They were flying. Slower than usual, but flying nonetheless. He looked at Amy. The wind was blowing her hair all over the place. Matt chuckled.

"This is amazing!" Amy exclaimed, giggling.

Matt concentrated on flying, but continued to steal glances at her, as she held on tight. Seeing Amy smiling like that, her deep brown eyes sparkling beneath the goggles, and her hair blowing around her heart-shaped face, Matt couldn't help but smile. Gosh, she's beautiful, he thought, before pushing the thought out of his head. They're friends, he reminded himself. It was best not to complicate things and risk ruining that friendship.

Amy's giggling suddenly stopped. Her smile abruptly faded.

"Are you okay?" Matt asked, full of concern, secretly wondering if she could read his thoughts. That was ridiculous, of course, but the thought crossed his mind nonetheless.

Amy pointed to a blue pillar of light across the East River. "What's that?" she asked. Everyone knew that two blue pillars, the "Tribute in Lights" are shined in the sky on September 11th every year, but this was in the middle of the spring.

"That's odd," said Matt. "Let's go check it out."

Amy held on to Matt as they flew toward the blue beam of light, neither of them sure of what to expect.

CHAPTER THIRTY-TWO

Matt and Amy were nearing the source of the beam of light, which appeared to originate on the top of a rather tall building, although by Manhattan standards the height was more or less average.

As they skimmed above the skyscrapers, Amy shivered. It was cold, being so high up with the wind whipping in her face. She wished she had brought her jacket. How was she supposed to know she'd be flying today? She clung on to Matt tighter, squeezing him. The leathery suit was warm against her body.

There was a silhouette, a tall, lanky man in a coat, standing in front of the light projector, the brightness of the beam obscuring his face. As the man noticed Spark, he pulled out what looked like a car clicker and pressed it. The light suddenly turned off, just as Matt landed.

Without the blinding light, Matt could begin to make out his features. The man was middle-aged, had thick, bushy eyebrows that desperately needed to be shaved, and a small blond goatee, neatly trimmed, along with a matching blond mess of thinning hair. His jaw was square, his chin contained a cleft, and there was a small scar just beneath his eye.

Amy suddenly felt scared and regretted coming. She began wishing she were home instead, for all the good that did her. Matt opened his mouth, about to ask the man what he was doing here, and what was the purpose of the light, but the man began talking before Matt could get a word out.

"Hello, Spark! I'm glad I have your attention. I was wondering when you'd get here," he said smiling, as if he knew him. "I'm the Inventor, perhaps you remember me?" He paused for dramatic effect, like he had an audience watching. "Oh, wait, you wouldn't remember me, because you're a *fake*, aren't you? Don't bother denying, I-"

He paused, suddenly, just noticing Amy for the first time. "Who is this? A sidekick?" he asked, surprised. "Lady, goggles are the worst disguise ever. You might as well just wear a pair of glasses!"

Amy felt uncomfortable, so much so that she forgot she should have been feeling afraid. She didn't like being the center of attention.

"She's not my sidekick," Matt said in a defensive tone. "And how did y—"

The Inventor exploded. "You brought your girlfriend here?! A civilian? Are you crazy!?! What if I had been a supervillain?" he yelled, before adding, "Well, I am, but what if this had been a trap? She'd be dead!"

Matt and Amy looked down at the floor, ashamed. Amy made sure to stick close to Matt's side.

"She's not my girlfriend," Matt mumbled, as if that was a defense. Then, louder, "Look, I'm new at this."

"Yes, of course you are. That's partly why I called you here. I lost a worthy adversary. I'd like to know what became of him. Why he stopped playing our little game."

"He died," Matt said, matter-of-factly.

"Hm. Killed?"

Matt sighed. "No, it was a car accident."

"An accident?" asked the Inventor, rhetorically. "Don't be so sure."

Matt's interest was certainly piqued. "What do you mean?"

"I think he may have been murdered," said the Inventor, as though he was discussing the weather. "He was being followed in the weeks before his disappearance. I have proof."

He held out a flash drive. Matt took it slowly, unable to say anything, still trying to process the new information.

"I have cameras throughout the city," the Inventor continued. "There's someone in the shadows on that footage, following Spark. Stalking him."

"Why?" Matt managed to choke out.

"He had a lot of enemies," said the Inventor, before pausing for a second. "Or did you mean to ask why I'm giving it to you? Well, as I said, I viewed him as a worthy adversary, and I think you, as his successor, deserve it. Besides, I'm trying to turn over a new leaf, as it were."

Matt looked at the flash drive in his palm, speechless.

"There's another thing," the Inventor continues. "Something's been on my mind lately. I made a mistake, and people got hurt. It's been eating me up inside, and I have no one to talk to about it." He sighed. "Spark was the closest thing I had to a friend, and you're not even him."

The Inventor looked at Spark who was studying the flash drive, obliviously. Whatever the Inventor had said seemed to have gone one ear and out the other.

Amy looked at Matt nervously, before stepping forward. She could see the pain on the Inventor's face.

"Hey," she said. "You can talk to me if you want."

The Inventor paused, unsure, then shrugged. "Do you believe in hell?" he asked. "Because if it exists, I'm going." His voice cracked at the end.

Amy thought for a moment. "I believe we each make our own hell, to an extent. We make choices in life, and we have to live with the choices we made. They haunt us forever. Those nights you can't sleep? That's your hell. And you'll carry it with you, day after day, as long as you're alive. You'll always have to live with the knowledge of what you've done, and you should, but that doesn't mean you can't make amends, it doesn't mean you can't learn from your mistakes, and it doesn't mean you can't move forward."

The Inventor nodded silently for a moment, before saying, "Yes, I suppose that makes sense. You're a smart kid." He seemed surprised.

Amy beamed, glad that she could help someone out.

The Inventor sighed, then mumbled, "You know, maybe I'll turn myself in." He headed to the door leading inside the building. As he opened it, he turned to Amy.

"You know," he said as he closed the door, "You don't make such a bad sidekick after all."

She looked at Matt, hoping for approval of some sort, but he was still staring at his flash drive. She tapped on the shoulder. He jerked up, startled.

"We should go," Amy said.

Matt just nodded wordlessly and slipped the flash drive into his pocket. Amy grabbed on to him as he jumped off the building and took to the air. They flew back to Matt's house in silence.

CHAPTER THIRTY-THREE

Dan had shown up to school early again. He pondered the weather as he waited for Matt. It was chilly, and the skies were cloudy. If someone didn't know better, Dan thought, they'd assume it was late fall.

He felt a tap on his shoulder. He turned, expecting to see Matt when a fist hit him in the jaw. His vision exploded with white. Dan was hurt and confused. Rubbing his face, and grateful he decided to wear his contact lenses that day, Dan turned to face his attacker.

Steve. Of course.

Steve towered over him, laughing.

"What's your problem, man?" Dan exclaimed.

"What's your problem, man?" Steve imitated Dan in a squeaky voice, which Dan noted sounded nothing like him. "You're the problem. That's what your dad thought, anyway. How does it feel, knowing your dad left your mom because of you?"

Dan's blood began to boil. He glared at Steve with hatred.

Steve raised an eyebrow in amusement, then laughed as he walked off.

Dan noticed a rock on the ground, and contemplated throwing it at Steve's head. The thought was interrupted by a familiar voice.

"Dan!" Amy called, cheerily. "What's up?"

Dan turned to face her, but then looked at the ground. He was too upset to look at her smile now.

"Hey, what's wrong?" Amy asked, concerned.

Dan's face was crimson red. He felt hot all over and could feel his heart thumping far beyond the posted speed limit. Dan could feel himself beginning to well up, but forced himself to hold onto his anger instead.

"It's that jerk, Steve," he hissed. "I could kill him." He was whispering, trying to control his voice. Dan kicked the rock at his feet and watched it hit the fence, making a loud clang.

Amy grimaced. "Hey, summer's gonna be here soon enough, and he'll have graduated and you'll never have to see him again," Amy said, trying to cheer him up.

Dan shrugged. "That day can't come soon enough," Dan said, before trying to change the subject. He didn't like talking about his own problems. The more he talked about them the more upset he became. "So where's Matt?"

"Oh, that reminds me!" Amy exclaimed. She took Dan's phone out of her pocket. "Matt wanted me to return this for him. He's not coming in today."

"Why not?" Dan said, confused. "He did tell you about the trunk, right?"

"Oh, he told me," Amy said, trying hard to suppress her grin. "Then he took me flying."

"What?! How was it?"

"Oh, it was amazing," Amy replied. "But that's not all that happened last night."

Dan opened his mouth to say something, but Amy quickly cut him off.

"Not that! Ew!" she said, glaring at him. "C'mon, get your head out of the gutter!"

Dan chuckled.

Amy then proceeded to talk excitedly, telling Dan about the events of the previous night.

Dan, however, only caught every few words. He began seething with jealousy, though he did his best not to show it. He was jealous of Amy, for going flying with Matt, and worried that maybe bringing Amy into the secret made him less special. He was also jealous of Matt, for being Spark, when Dan knew he could do a better job himself.

What made Matt so special anyway? Dan knew more about superheroes than Matt ever would! Heck, Evan got along with Dan better than he ever did with Matt! The suit should've rightfully been his!

Amy was oblivious to all this, talking enthusiastically with a smile on her face about her experience soaring through the clouds. Dan pushed his feelings down and flashed a smile, a fairly convincing one at that. Dan *knew* he was destined for great things. He wouldn't just be a sidekick. He'd prove himself. He knew he was special, and eventually, everyone else would know that too.

Matt sat alone in his dark room. He had been looking at the footage for hours, studying it, hoping it would give some sort of clue. All of the recordings were of the same three weeks, each one marked with the date and time. Some of the videos had Spark running on rooftops before jumping off and flying away, and some just had Spark fly by. Every one of them had someone in the shadows, watching. Waiting.

For what? Matt wondered. He looked closely. The grainy footage made it impossible to make out any identifying marks. It was a man though, that Matt was sure of. He yawned and tried to wipe the sleep from his eyes. Realizing there was nothing more to do with the footage, Matt got up and headed to the shower.

After getting dressed, Matt reached for his phone, only to remember he had given it to Dan to look at. Suddenly he remembered he still had Evan's phone. He raced to his draw and pulled it open. It was still here.

He turned on the phone, confirming it was still in service. Matt slipped it into his pocket as he left the house, hoping a walk would clear his head and yield new leads. As he walked, he thought about the events of the previous night.

Perhaps I should've tried to arrest the Inventor, he thought, but pushed the thought out of his mind. The Inventor gave him the opportunity to avenge his brother, to get closure. *You can't put a price on that*, Matt thought.

He began to wonder what he would even do once he found the guy. Kill him? No, Matt knew he wasn't a killer. Arrest him? But he probably knows Evan's secret and could expose it, putting the whole Stone family in danger. Matt scowled. It would be worth that price to bring his brother's killer to justice. His blood boiled. Nearly anything would be worth the price.

Suddenly, something began buzzing his pocket. Matt reached in and pulled out Evan's vibrating phone. It was an alarm reminding Evan he had a criminology class in ten minutes. Matt recalled Evan had a friend in that class who had shown up for the funeral, Eric-something. Matt shrugged, reasoning that was as good a lead as any, and began trekking toward Brooklyn College.

CHAPTER THIRTY-FOUR

After Matt reached the college he noticed a security guard at the gate looking at college IDs. His heart skipped a beat. No, he wasn't going to be turned away for something as mundane as this, he decided.

Matt took out his transportation card which he normally used for riding the train, and flashed it to the guard as he walked in. He nervously broke into a brisk walk, hoping the guard wouldn't catch on and call him back for a closer look. Luckily the guard was too busy devouring a croissant to notice.

As Matt looked around the quad full of students milling about, he found he had trouble finding the building or room he was looking for. Oh, Evan's phone had the corresponding building letter and room number, but the building names didn't seem to match the letters. It was all so confusing. There seemed no rhyme or reason to the layout.

A few students were sitting on a bench nearby, and Matt noticed a number of people sitting around in circles on the emerald green grass, talking in an animated fashion. He thought of going over to one of them to ask for directions, but thought better of it. If someone found out he didn't belong, Matt could find himself kicked out.

At the end of the quad was a bell tower that housed the library, as evidenced by the big sign overhead. After walking through the heavy wooden doors into the lobby, he saw the information desk through the glass doors leading into the next room.

Matt attempted to go through them, but was stopped by a uniformed guard who insisted Matt show him his student ID before passing through. Why the guard insisted on ID when hypothetically, Matt already showed it to get onto the campus, Matt didn't understand. A long haired man walked past Matt, showing his ID, which the guard took and studied before letting the man through. Matt knew the transportation card trick wouldn't work again. Dejected, Matt exited the building and sat on the stone stoop.

Eventually, a kind, freckled redhead took pity on Matt and pointed him towards James Hall, which was confusingly across the street. It appeared the college campus was literally cut in half. After sneaking past a guard posted at the gate across the street using the transportation card again, Matt finally found the correct room and waited outside for the class to end.

He began running through in his head how the conversation would go, over and over. When the class finally began to empty, so did Matt's head. He spotted Eric, a large, heavy fellow with olive skin, long dark hair dyed with streaks of green, and a trimmed beard. A tattoo of what was either a bat or demon peeked out of his left sleeve. Frankly, he wasn't hard to spot.

"Hey, Eric!" Matt called out, unsure of where the conversation would go from there.

"Hm?" Eric looked confused. "Can I help you?" he asked.

"I'm Matt, Evan's brother?" Matt said, as though he was unsure.

"Oh, yeah, we met!" Eric said, a look of realization on his face. "How're you holding up?"

Matt shrugged. "Can I asked you a few questions?"

"You already are, little man," Eric said with a laugh. Matt smiled uncomfortably. "You mind if we walk while we talk?"

Matt nodded "So, how well did you know Evan?"

"Pretty well, I'd say," Eric replied. "I mean, the guy didn't have a lot of close friends, I'd say I was one of the few. It helped that we had a similar interest."

"Criminology?"

"Well, yeah, that and superheroes. I've actually got a poster of a screenshot from that video of Dragonfly stopping that bank heist that was all over the internet last year."

"Cool," Matt said. "Evan was always partial to Spark though."

"Yeah, Evan was always trying to convince me Spark was the better hero." Eric paused, as he thought for a moment. "I suppose it's because Spark's more mysterious. There's only one clear picture of him, and he's never done any interviews or anything. The last few weeks before, you know," he looked at Matt with pity, "he

161

insisted that all that was going to change. That Spark's time in the shadows were at an end."

"What'd you think of that?"

"Honestly, I didn't believe him. Besides, I think Spark's better off in the shadows. Easier to help people that way. But Evan always acted like he knew best."

Matt nodded in understanding.

"Well, I gotta run! Work, you know."

"Okay. Oh, and thanks for talking to me. I'm still trying to make sense of it all, you know?" Eric bobbed his head. "Yeah."

"Oh, by the way, where do you work?"

"My uncle's auto repair shop," Eric said proudly, and he turned away. "Nice talking to you!"

Matt waved halfheartedly. "You too," he managed to choke out.

Matt's head was spinning. It couldn't be that Eric would kill Matt, could it? Sure, he had the means, but there wasn't a motive, as far as he knew. Unless he found out Evan was Spark and killed him out of jealousy. Matt shook his head. No, that didn't make sense. But *someone* was stalking Spark, and at the moment Eric was the only suspect Matt had.

He sat down on a bench, trying to calm down. His pocket buzzed. Evan's phone. Again. Matt took it out and turned off the alarm. This one was for a criminal justice class. With no better leads, Matt headed back into the building, hoping this classroom would be easier to find than the last.

As he approached the classroom, students were filing in. Matt stopped, unsure of how to proceed. Does he walk into the classroom and ask the class if anyone knew Evan? Ask each person individually as they walk out? And what did he hope to gain from this? Matt sighed as he realized his plan wasn't well thought out.

Someone touched his shoulder. Already on edged, Matt instantly turned around. In front of him, with her backpack swung over her shoulder, was a girl. She had straight bleached blonde hair which, considering her jet black eyebrows, was obviously not her natural hair color. Her eyes were a piercing bright blue, and her round face had an orange tint, as though she adorned herself with too much self-tanning lotion.

She's beautiful, Matt thought, completely forgetting in the moment why he was there.

"What're you doing here? Are you, like, stalking me?" Her hands were on her hips, and she had a distinct Russian accent.

The question startled Matt. "Stalk you? I don't know you."

"Well, it certainly looks like you are. I'm taking Crim, and I saw you creeping around there too. Now, should I like, call the campus police, or what?" she said, arms crossed.

Matt sighed with frustration. "My name's Matt," he said as he extended his hand. "Evan was my brother. Evan Stone?"

"Omigosh! You're Evan's little brother, I can like, totally see it!" the girl said excitingly. "I'm Anna, bee-tee-doubleyou." A look of concern quickly washed over her face as the realization hit her. "Oh, I'm so sorry about Evan. It was such a shame. He was a total cutie."

Anna had a look of genuine concern on her face, but Matt wondered why some people didn't think before they opened their mouths. "Mhm," was all he could say in response.

"So why are you here? Can I help?" she looked at her watch.

"Are you late to class?" Matt asked, concerned.

"Oh, that doesn't really matter, I can be a little late," Anna said laughing.

"Well, did you know Evan? Were you friends?"

"Oh, yeah. I mean, not well, but we like, spoke and stuff. I totally would've asked him out if I didn't already have a bee-eff, you know?" Matt nodded. "Now that green-haired guy, Aaron or Eric or something, he was close with Evan."

Matt nodded again. "Yeah, we've already met."

"I wonder how he's holding up. I mean, I know I'd be like, majorly depressed if the last thing I ever did with my bee-eff-eff was fight, you know?" Anna said, looking like she was deep in thought.

Matt's ears perked up. "Fight? What fight?"

"I don't know, they were like, yelling at each other in the hall, and then Evan stormed off."

"Do you remember what it was about?" Matt asked earnestly.

"Not really," Anna said quickly. "Look, Matt, it was awesome to meet you, but I really have to get to class. Don't be a stranger though!"

She winked at him before walking into the classroom. Matt blushed for a moment, before remembering why he was there. So Eric had lied to him, or at the very least left something out. Whatever they were fighting about made an impression on Anna.

As Matt stood there alone, in an empty hall, he knew he had to get to the bottom of it.

CHAPTER THIRTY-FIVE

This time the dream was different. There was no car. Instead, Matt was standing in the middle of Times Square. He looked around.

Deserted.

Something flew overhead. Spark. Matt began chasing him. Ahead, a dark figure was chasing Spark too. Matt tried to catch up, but felt as though he was moving in molasses. His legs had stopped working properly and he fell to the ground. Matt began crawling, desperately trying to catch up to the dark figure. But as he crawled, he got slower and slower. He reached out his hand grazing the leg of his adversary. The figure stopped, and slowly, menacingly, turned around.

Matt awoke suddenly. Bright light met his eyes. Someone was holding his shoulder, shaking him. Matt wiped the drool from his lower lip as he looked up.

It was a security guard. He had fallen asleep on a bench outside the college, where he'd been thinking. The security guard looked upset.

"You're not allowed to sleep here."

"Sorry," Matt mumbled. "I didn't get much sleep last night."

His head was spinning. As Matt got up and began walking away, he glanced at Evan's phone. He'd been sleeping for at least an hour and a half. Matt wondered if he already missed his opportunity to question Eric. It abruptly occurred to Matt that Eric's number might be in his brother's phone. He began looking through Evan's contacts. It didn't take long to find. There was only one Eric, an Eric Reese. Matt dialed and raised the phone to his ear. After what seemed like an eternity, Eric picked up.

"Hey, don't do that, kid. You freaked me out for a second when your brother's number came up." He sounded upset.

"Sorry," Matt replied. "My phone broke, so I've been using his."

"Uh-huh, make it quick, I gotta get back to work," Eric said brusquely.

"Um, I just wanted to ask you about the last time you saw Evan. I heard there was a fight?" There was a long pause. "Eric?"

"Yeah, sorry. Yeah, we fought. I feel kinda guilty about it."

Matt nodded. Then it occurred to him that Eric couldn't see him. "I understand," he said quickly, before adding, "What did you guys fight about?"

"Nothing really, it was stupid. He said he had a secret, but he wasn't sure if he should share it with me yet. I don't remember exactly what happened, I guess I got upset. Then Evan said he'd share it with someone who would appreciate it and stormed off." Eric paused for a moment before adding, "Hey, who told you about this anyway?"

"Oh, um, some girl," Matt replied. "Anna, I think her name was."

"Oh." Eric sounded surprised. "I wonder if *she* was his secret. Those two were awfully friendly. I mean, she had a boyfriend, but I've seen her and Evan flirting before." He paused before quickly saying, "Listen, I really gotta go. Take care, kid."

Matt walked, alone with his thoughts. So Evan had a secret, which was probably that he was Spark, but if he did have a secret girlfriend, maybe she knew about it. Maybe she was the reason he got killed? To hide the relationship? Or she was secretly an assassin? Or maybe her boyfriend was involved in the Russian mob?

Matt's mind raced through the possibilities, plausible and ridiculous alike. It began to dawn on him just how little he knew about Evan. His head started to spin. Matt felt drained. He was tired of sleuthing. There were so many theories and no way to prove any of them. He suddenly felt unsure of everything.

The final bell had rung. School had finally let out. Dan and Amy met outside.

"I'm worried about Matt," Dan said, a concerned look on his face. "I thought he would've at least shown up halfway through the day. He's missed over a week of school this semester already."

"He's just working through some stuff," Amy said, rather dismissively. "He just needs time."

Dan thought again that *he* should've been the one wearing the Spark suit. Matt plainly wasn't seeing things clearly, and his obsessing over his brother's death made him incompetent. Matt didn't have what it took to be a hero, Dan knew. Not like *he* could be.

Dan was shoved, snapping him out of his string of thought. He stumbled as he got up. He heard Steve laughing in the background as he walked away.

"That jerk," Amy said, upset, giving Steve's back a death-glare. She turned to Dan. "Don't worry, his life probably peaked three weeks ago. Ten years from now and he'll be working for you."

But Dan couldn't hear her. He was staring at Steve, blood boiling, seething with anger. He imagined himself in the Spark suit, charging at Steve. Spark punched him. Steve flew ten feet, smashing into a bus with a sickening thud, denting it. Spark leaped over to Steve, landing mere inches from him. He lifted Steve with one hand, as Steve cried, begged for mercy. Spark punched him repeatedly. Within seconds, Steve's face was more blood than skin. Gasps were heard all around. Spark looked up, seeing Amy's and Rose's horrified faces. He dropped Steve, and looked in shock at his own bloody hands.

"Dan?"

Dan snapped back to reality. "Hm?"

"I said he's not worth it," Amy said, looking at Dan, her brow furrowed in concern.

Dan forced a smile. "Yeah, you're right," he said.

As they began walking and Amy turned away, a look of worry began to grow on Dan's face. His little daydream alarmed him.

Maybe I'm better off without the suit, he thought.

CHAPTER THIRTY-SIX

Matt had been home for only a few minutes when there was a knock on the door. He looked through the peephole and unlocked the door. Dan and Amy barged in.

"I'm sorry," Amy said apologetically as Matt slowly closed the door. "I said you needed some space. But Dan insisted we come anyway." She shot Dan a look.

Matt smirked. Dan gave Matt a wide grin. "I come bearing gifts!" he said in his best mock-British accent, lifting up a pile of papers. "Your homework, good sir!"

"Gee, thanks," Matt said, trying to hold a deadpan expression, but failing.

In all of the events of the past eighteen hours, he'd forgotten how good it felt to be surrounded by friends. The three of them together just felt simple, unlike the rest of his life. It felt right. He was glad he told Amy. Matt chuckled.

"I also have," Dan paused as he struggled to take something out of his pockets, "your dead-as-a-doornail cell phone!" Dan finished as he produced the phone from his pockets.

Matt took it. "So you couldn't fix it?"

"Nope. It's fried. Even the SIM card is useless, due to the integrated circuits within the identification module being burned beyond repair."

Matt nodded, pretending he understood what that meant.

"I still have no idea how your suit still works after being affected by even a weak, localized electromagnetic pulse. By all accounts, it shouldn't."

Matt shrugged.

"Wait!" Amy said, alarmed, turning to Dan. "How're we supposed to reach Matt?"

Matt held up Evan's phone. "I found Evan's phone today, so I guess I'll use that. You guys have the number, right?"

The two nodded.

By this point, the trio had made their way to the purple-and-gold couch in the living room. Amy and Dan sat down, while Matt took the armchair across from them. His relaxed demeanor that had been there seconds ago faded as he leaned forward.

"So I've been doing some digging today," he began. "Evan mentioned in his journals he thought he was being followed. I've seen the footage. Someone was definitely stalking Evan, and I think whoever it was found out his secret identity. The car accident wasn't an accident."

"Are you sure?" Amy asked.

"I asked the mechanic a while ago when I first suspected it, and he said it *is* possible. I pushed it out of my mind for a while, because I knew it was unlikely, but

172

the footage last night proves someone *was* stalking Evan."

Dan interrupted. "Or at the very least, someone stalked Spark. He or she might not have known it was Evan."

Matt paused. "True," he said, finally. "But whoever it was obviously found out and sabotaged the car."

"Unless that's unrelated," Dan said, interrupting again.

"It still could've been an accident, right?" Amy asked, finding it necessary to add in her own two cents.

Matt began to grow frustrated. "No, it wasn't. It couldn't have been! It's too convenient for someone to be stalking Evan and for him to die a little later. It can't be a coincidence!" By the end of the sentence, Matt was practically yelling.

Amy and Dan looked uncomfortable.

Matt closed his eyes for a second to calm down. "Look, I've been doing some research, and have a few suspects."

Amy's and Dan's interest seemed piqued. They leaned forward in their seats.

Matt continued, confidently. "So Evan had a friend, Eric Reese, who was really into superheroes. And people saw them arguing, shortly before Evan died." Matt hesitated. It still wasn't easy to just say that. "They were arguing about a secret that Evan had."

"Presumably that he was Spark," Dan said, interrupting yet again. Matt glared at him.

"Yes, presumably that he was Spark. So anyway, this Eric guy works at an auto body shop. He's got the ability, and possibly the knowledge and motive. I don't know, I'm still working on it."

"We can't do anything without proof," Amy said, matter-of-factly.

Matt nodded. "There's another suspect. A girl, Anna. Supposedly she and Evan were an item, despite her having a boyfriend. Oh, and she was aware of him having a secret, though I don't know if she knew what it was."

"Well I'm sure a possible romance in the mix could be a motive, either for her or her boyfriend, depending on the situation, but I don't see how the Spark angle fits in." Dan rubbed his forehead.

"Well, it *has* to, somehow. I mean, *someone* was following him," Matt said, his eyes intense. "I've seen the footage. It has to be tied to Evan's..." He paused again, unable to bring himself to say it. "It has to be tied to what happened to him." Matt sighed. "Look, I'm not an idiot. *Maybe*, yeah, maybe it was just an accident. A coincidence of timing. Whatever. But that doesn't change that we still have footage of *someone* following Spark. Someone knew who he was. Or was trying to. And we have to get to the bottom of it." He exhaled, and it only then occurring to him he'd been holding his breath, before whispering to himself the last bit. "I have to get to the bottom of it."

"Let's see the footage," Dan replied. "Maybe I'll be able to play around with the contrast or brightness or whatever, and we can see who it is."

Amy made a face. "Well, I'll just be useless. I'm meeting a friend tonight anyway. You'll keep me updated though, right?"

Matt and Dan nodded and said goodbye to Amy as she left.

Dan and Matt were up in Matt's room. Dan fiddled around with Matt's computer, hoping it could tell them something they didn't already know. Matt knew another reason was that Dan didn't want to go home, but he didn't say anything.

"You know," Matt said, as Dan worked silently. "This doesn't seem clean at all. Like, I half-expected all the clues to line up, and I'd solve this in a couple of days or something. But this just seems like, well, like a mess."

Dan didn't answer, as he looked at the screen intently. Matt didn't think Dan even heard him. Not that it mattered. Matt knew he was just talking things out for his own benefit anyway. He was simply trying to just make sense of it all.

"That's because this isn't a movie or TV show," Dan suddenly responded, a few moments late.

So he'd been listening after all.

Dan spoke slowly, as though his attention was elsewhere. Which it was. "There isn't a writer here, who lines up perfect clues that all make sense. This isn't Sherlock Holmes or CSI. This is real life. And real life is sloppy. It rarely makes sense."

Matt gave a sort of half-grunt in response.

Dan turned around to face him. "You know, over one-third of all murders in the U.S. are never solved, right? And even the ones that are, it can take months or even years." He turned back to the computer and began clicking. "Television gives us false expectations," he mumbled. "It's ruining America, I think."

Matt grunted in agreement.

Dan opened his mouth again to speak. He hesitated, as if unsure. Finally, he spoke. "Maybe the two aren't related."

"What? What two things? What do you mean?" Matt asked confused.

Evan's death and the person following him."

"What are you saying?!" Matt asked angrily. "Are you insinuating that it was just an accident? Are you saying I killed him?"

"Well, it does seem to be the simplest—"

"No," Matt said cutting him off. "Evan didn't die because of my driving. It was sabotage. It had to be. I didn't kill him."

Dan nodded, realizing he'd taken it too far. "Well, it was your mother's car. Maybe someone wanted her dead?"

"And it's just a coincidence that they killed Spark, one of New York's greatest heroes?" Matt asked rhetorically. "No, I don't think so. Besides, I looked into it already. My mother had no enemies."

"That you know of," Dan mumbled, a little too loud.

"This video is proof." Mat insisted. "Someone wanted him dead. This is the only explanation."

Dan didn't answer.

A few minutes of awkward silence later, Dan slumped back in his chair. "Alright, that's as good as we're gonna get."

Matt leaned in, eyes on the screen. There was a window open containing a video player that took up most of the space. Dan pressed the 'play' icon at the bottom of the window.

The video was zoomed in, and while still grainy, it was brighter than it was before. It was very pixelated, however, and while a basic body type could be made out of the silhouette, it still wasn't as clear as Matt had hoped. The figure was small and thin, but it was still difficult to tell if it was male or female.

"I guess we can rule out Eric. He's too big." Matt looked at it closer, squinting his eyes. "Can you, like, make it less boxy?" Matt asked, referring to the pixels.

Dan rolled his eyes. "Matt, again, this isn't a TV show. The video is in a specific resolution. The bigger I make it, the more pixelated it becomes." He paused the video. "And that's the best picture I can get out of it!" he added, exasperated.

177

"Hm. So we're back to square one?" Matt was upset. He wanted answers. He wanted someone to blame.

"No, we know someone was following Spark, and we know that it wasn't Eric. It still might've been that Anna girl. The videos are time-stamped, so maybe try to see if she's got an alibi for that time?"

"Yeah, I guess that makes sense. And maybe I'll head to where the videos were recorded, see if maybe there are any clues or whatever."

"It's a long shot," Dan said, matter of factly.

"I know."

They both sat there awkwardly for a few moments. Matt didn't know how to ask Dan to leave tactfully. Dan picked up on it a few moments after he should have.

"So, uh, I guess I'll head out. Got, y'know, homework and stuff."

"Yeah," Matt replied, nodding perhaps a bit too much. "I'll call you if I go patrol tonight."

"Cool."

Dan headed downstairs. After a few more awkward pleasantries, he headed out the door. As Matt closed the door, something occurred to him. Eric had mentioned that Evan had said he would only share his secret with "Someone who would appreciate it." He recalled Evan using similar words when talking about Dan, and their mutual love of superheroes.

A chill went up Matt's spine.

Maybe Evan told Dan his secret.

But if Dan already knew, why would he act like he didn't? Could he be the one who sabotaged the car? He's certainly smart enough to figure that out. Matt tried to force the unsettling thought out of his mind. No, that couldn't be right. That didn't make sense. What would Dan's motive be anyway? And Matt knew Dan for years. There's no way he'd do something like that.

Besides, thought Matt, finally convincing himself, *even if Evan told Dan, it still wouldn't explain who was following him around.* Why would someone who already knew Evan's secret follow him around anyway?

On the other hand, Dan sure did seem to be trying to convince him to look elsewhere. He didn't even want Matt to go back to the scene where Evan was being followed. It seemed as though Dan wanted Matt to think that Evan's death was just a tragic car accident, or perhaps had to do with his mother. And he *claimed* he couldn't make the picture of who followed Evan any clearer, but that doesn't make it true. He could be protecting himself. It would make sense, in a way.

Matt knew Dan always wanted to be a superhero. Maybe he thought getting Evan out of the way would open up the opportunity for him to get the Spark suit? Did that mean he was biding his time to steal the suit from Matt? Or worse, Dan's simply waiting for the opportunity to kill him and *take* the suit.

It makes sense. It all makes sense.

Matt felt sick to his stomach. His head began to swim. Dan. His best friend. Matt began to sweat. He hated this. He hated being so unsure about everything.

Matt looked out the window. He needed to clear his head. It was a cloudy, chilly night, but he didn't care. He needed fresh air.

He needed to fly.

CHAPTER THIRTY-SEVEN

A man awoke. He couldn't sleep. Then again, this wasn't unusual. He always had trouble sleeping. The room was sterile and smelled like a doctor's office. Other than the bed, draped with steel-gray sheets, and a simple metallic lamp, the room was unfurnished. He didn't feel the need to surround himself with frivolous things. The necessities do just fine.

The man got out of his lonely king-sized bed, and walked across the polished floor of the unadorned room to the wall-sized window, which overlooked the skyline. Rain gently tapped against it as a few streams slowly raced each other to the bottom. His bare chest slowly rose and fell as he closed his eyes, controlling his breathing. His eyelids slowly lifted.

Looking at his mirrored reflection in the window, he observed the build of his body. It looked like that of a Greek god, but that didn't matter to him. Not much did anymore. He heaved a sigh. The man ran his hands through his long, thick golden hair, which rested on his thin, angular face. As he gazed through the window, the man surveyed the city laid out before him.

A pity, he thought. America used to be great, once. And New York was its crown jewel. Now look at what's become of it. It has let itself become a shell of what it once was. Corruption, crime, poverty, it all runs rampant now across the city. His city.

And flourishing in his city was the worst sin of all: ignorance.

Stupidity.

Contentment.

The man's face curled in disgust and revulsion. The schools have become a cesspool of wanton idiocy and inanity. This city once produced the greatest minds. Now look at it. Even the politicians, once brilliant, wallowed in the filth of the uneducated. Treating them as equals. The thought was sickening.

He sighed. The man knew that the city could fashion great minds again. The city, the country, wasn't lost. Not entirely. Not yet.

The man glared downward at his beloved city below, as though she were an old adversary or an old lover. The two aren't all that different, after all. His bright green eyes stared, unblinking. He could feel the metropolis staring up at him, daring to make the next move. And he was getting there. He was almost ready. Soon.

He knew he would never sleep well. Not until he rectified the problem. Not until he saved his city.

Rain poured down, making the music of thousands of tiny drums as the droplets hit the ground in a symphony of unending fury. A dark figure walked by.

The disheveled man had a lot on his mind as he limped along down the street, not even bothering to avoid the puddles. Jenny-Lynn, his girlfriend-- well, she was actually his friend Rob's girlfriend, had just told him that she needed money for beauty school, and was threatening to tell Rob about their secret relationship if he didn't give her the money she needed. And as if he didn't have enough on his mind, he still owed Big Stan a solid two G's for flushing the product the other day when he thought the police were at the door.

At least he had jury duty. At forty bucks a day, he should have that money back in... well his math wasn't the greatest, but he knew he should have the money soon enough. He hoped Jenny-Lynn wouldn't tell Rob before then. He didn't need *another* cap in his leg.

Rain ran down his pointed nose and gaunt cheeks, dripping to the street below. His face was full of lines, making the man look far older than he was, and he looked like he hadn't shaved in days. The man ran his hand through his wet, already graying hair, as he thought about his lot in life, and wondered how he could turn it around. The brooding man came to the conclusion he should buy a lottery ticket. He determined *that* would certainly fix his problems. He began to dream of all he would buy with the money that, in his mind, was already his.

A car drove by, spraying him with mud and water. He cursed as he pulled up his hood, wondering why he wasn't wearing it before. He paused, realizing he had reached his destination.

The hooded man stopped in front of the bookstore. He was waiting for someone. The man took out his watch. He liked to tell people it was a family heirloom. And it was. It just wasn't *his* family.

He checked the time. No. He was late. *Again.* Big Stan was going to have his head.

The man looked up to the sky. He wasn't religious in any sense, yet he found himself praying to someone, anyone who would listen. Rain washed across his face, into his eyes, mouth, and down into his clothes. He scanned the heavens, hoping, waiting for a sign. He cursed.

High above him flew a hero. Even in the rain, he could make out the black and blue, with the shock of blond hair against the dark building across from him. It could only be Spark.

He ran.

CHAPTER THIRTY-EIGHT

It was a cloudy day out, but the weather was mild. Comfortable. Most of the rain from the night before had dried up, leaving little pools of water, like miniature ponds, scattered about. Matt sat alone on a swing in the schoolyard, holding a plastic container full of rice and what he could only assume was a certain kind of meat. He decided to eat lunch outside today. Matt wasn't trying to avoid anyone, he simply felt too claustrophobic indoors today.

Matt remembered that it was Thursday, which meant Amy would be meeting with the other girls in her softball team to discuss the upcoming season. Amy was the pitcher with a great arm, which from Matt's limited knowledge of softball made her pretty important to the team. He and Dan would occasionally go to a game or two every season to support her, although they mostly found themselves bored. It was amusing to Matt that out of the three of them, the most athletically inclined one was the only girl. But if Amy was with her team now, that meant she wasn't spending lunch with Dan.

The thought of Dan sitting alone popped into Matt's head. He still had to play it cool until he was sure. He couldn't tip Dan off that he was onto him. Matt quickly texted Dan to let him know where he was. A few minutes later, Dan showed up.

"You know, I was just about to ask Rose out when I got your text. Guess it'll have to wait," he said, smirking.

Matt rolled his eyes, but couldn't suppress his smile. Maybe he was wrong about Dan. Maybe he was just jumping to conclusions.

"You're always 'just about' to ask her out."

"And one of these days I will, if you wouldn't keep interrupting me," he said jokingly. Dan sat down on the swing next to Matt. "So I hear you were busy last night. Guess you don't need my help anymore." He sounded bitter, although it looked like he was trying to hide it. He wasn't doing a very good job.

Matt looked at Dan confused. "I honestly have no idea what you're talking about."

"You went out last night. And I never got a phone call. Whatever. It's fine." He tried not to sound hurt.

"Listen, it was only for a few minutes. I needed to clear my head." Matt looked at the ground. "I don't think I've been thinking straight lately."

"Hmph. 'Only for a few minutes,'" Dan repeated. "You were out until four in the morning. How are you not tired?"

"What!?!" Matt exclaimed, more confused than ever. "I went to sleep before midnight! What are you talking about?"

Dan looked unconvinced. "Are you sure?"

"Of course I'm sure! What kind of question is that?"

Dan took out his phone and began typing something on it. "I think you should see this," he said, holding out his phone.

Matt looked at the screen. It was one of those superhero gossip sites. Apparently, there had been a Spark sighting at four in the morning last night, along with a blurry picture taken by the eyewitness. Matt squinted, trying to get a better look at the image. It was slightly out of focus, and the picture was taken while it was raining, but it certainly looked like Spark.

Matt turned back to Dan. "That's not me. I mean, it looks like me, but it's not. I was sleeping. I swear."

Matt wondered if he was going crazy. Could it have been him, sleepwalking or something, and he just doesn't remember? Was the stress of everything finally taking its toll?

"Hm," Dan replied, looking back at the picture. "Then I guess it's a hoax. They're not *that* uncommon."

"A hoax? Is that possible?"

"Yeah, it wouldn't be too hard." Dan chuckled. "I've thought about doing it once or twice. A similar thing happened last year. Rumors were floating around about a hero named Darkblood, though the whole thing turned out to be a prank by one guy. He used a remote control drone-helicopter-thingy, some tape, string, and a painted lightweight blowup dummy. It's pretty simple, actually."

Matt nodded, still unsure.

"Oh, by the way, you know the FalconTech tablets are coming out tomorrow!?!" Dan smiled as if it was his own accomplishment. "Our school is getting a shipment in the hundreds. I can't wait to get my hands on one!"

"Don't you work there? They have prototypes and stuff, right?"

"Oh, they've been very secretive. Barely anyone but Arthur Falcon gets to handle them." Dan went on to talk about the specific specs, expansion ports, graphics cards, processing power, and the like. He was clearly very excited.

Matt nodded as though he was listening. His mind was still on the Spark hoax. He couldn't help but wonder if it was connected to the person who was following Spark prior to Evan's death.

And so the plot thickens.

By the time Dan had finished talking, Matt was convinced that there had to be a connection. *And Dan seems to know an awful lot about it.*

"So explain this to me," Matt said, interrupting Dan. "You don't find it strange that someone's impersonating Spark, and that someone was following Evan, and that Evan died because of a sabotaged car—"

"You're still on this?" Dan said in a frustrated tone. "Listen to yourself! You're acting all paranoid! You just don't want to consider that it's possible the person responsible for your brother's death is *you!*"

"How dare you!" Matt yelled. "You're still trying to hide the truth. I didn't kill my brother. We *both* know that.

You've wanted to be a superhero since forever! So you stalked him, and sabotaged the car, knowing it would kill him, leaving you free to get the Spark suit—"

"You're crazy! Do you hear what you're saying?!"

Matt continued, his breathing heavy and his blood boiling as he struggled not to raise his voice. "But you didn't count on *me* surviving, did you? It through a wrench in your little scheme. So you've been trying to cover it up, planting thoughts in my head, trying to make me look elsewhere, and purposefully make it impossible to tell who it is on the video footage—"

"You've lost it. I don't have to listen to this!" Dan said as he stormed off.

Matt yelled in Dan's direction, "I'll prove it! I will! And when I do, I'm coming for you!"

Dan didn't turn around. A few people in the yard stared at Matt. That didn't matter. He'd prove he was right. And then he'd bring Dan to justice.

CHAPTER THIRTY-NINE

The sky was black and starless, as the nighttime Manhattan sky typically is. Flying didn't help clear his head. Not now. There was too much swimming around in it. He had to get to the bottom of this. He hadn't spoken to Dan since the afternoon. He couldn't. He could barely stand his *own* voice in his head at the moment, let alone the voice of his brother's killer. He wished he had played it cool though. Now Dan knew he was on to him.

That didn't matter though. Matt was still going to take him down. Doubts began to form in his head. If Dan's plan had been to get rid of both Evan and Matt, how could he have known Evan would take him driving that day? Matt pushed the thoughts out of his head. No, he was sure. It had to be Dan. Maybe he was working with someone else, but he had to be involved. Matt couldn't second-guess himself. He was right. And he would prove it.

The crisp air surrounded his body, pushing against his face as he cut through it. Matt saw one of the buildings up ahead. It was a residential building, made of faded red brick. It was a rather small building, as Manhattan buildings go. Most of the lights were off at this hour, but the building was still illuminated by the lights of surrounding buildings.

Matt's eyes scanned the roof. It looked exactly like the video, as if it was undisturbed in all that time. He landed on the concrete floor. It was uneven, he observed, glancing around, hoping to find something, anything, that could provide answers for him.

Nothing.

Suddenly, out of the corner of his eye, he saw a red dot. Turning quickly to face it, he noticed it blinking. Slowly. Methodically. Watching him. It took him a moment to realize what it was. The Inventor's camera. Of course. It was attached to a water tank, though it looked like it was glued on as opposed to screwed into place. He looked closer. For something that had braved the elements for so long, it seemed to be in remarkable condition.

Matt moved forward, grabbing it in frustration. The camera broke in his hands. He let the pieces fall to the floor. He stared at the remnants, plastic and wires, laying at his feet, as if maybe they had the answers. If only. If only there was another camera, another point of view. If only he had more to go on. He stopped breathing.

Of course! How could he not have thought of this earlier?

Matt reached into his pocket and pulled out Evan's phone. The one camera he had not yet checked. It had never occurred to him before then to look at the pictures saved on it. Perhaps they held a clue. Something that could help him make sense of all this.

Matt pressed the 'picture gallery' icon on the phone and began swiping through the pictures. At first, the pictures were just a few pictures of Matt and Evan, there were a few selfies of Evan as well, and a picture of him with a movie star, who, by the look of it, was filming something at Brooklyn College. The next picture caused Matt to pause.

It was a picture of Spark. Matt studied it. Something was off. It was a picture of him from the side, with the background indecipherable. It looked to be taken outside though. Evan shouldn't have a picture like this. It didn't make sense. The way he was standing, the way the picture was shot, it wasn't a selfie.

Matt's eyes swelled as the realization washed over him. Someone *else* must've taken this picture. And whoever it was, probably Dan, must've known Evan's secret. But if Evan had someone taking pictures of him in the suit, if he trusted someone enough to do that, why didn't he put it in the journal? If Evan and Dan shared the secret, why didn't Evan mention it anywhere?

Matt continued to swipe through the pictures. It was picture after picture of Spark, taken at various angles, some from behind, and quite a few of him flying.

Why didn't the person who took these come forward after Evan died? Especially when Spark started showing up again with Matt under the suit. Unless that person already knew that and didn't have Spark's best interest at heart. Because that person was the killer.

It was Dan. It *had* to be. That was the *only* explanation. Dan was the only one up until recently who knew Matt was under the suit. And he pushed for Matt to tell others, so he wouldn't be the only suspect. Matt's mind raced. This was still just circumstantial. He needed definitive proof.

Matt swiped to the next picture. His hands began shaking as his heart raced. The phone fell to the floor, clattering against the cement floor.

No, it was impossible. It didn't make sense.

The phone's screen had cracked, but the picture was still clear and bright, illuminating the space around it. Matt stared at it, a selfie of Evan, with Spark flying in the background.

Evan wasn't in the suit. Someone else was.

Matt began to make sense of it all. Evan's secret was that he discovered Spark's secret identity. Evan was *never* Spark.

Evan was the stalker.

CHAPTER FORTY

Matt felt sick. His heart began to pound hard and fast. He pulled off the mask as he began hyperventilating.

Evan was never Spark at all. It was all a lie. The reason Matt was flying around, risking his life— Evan's legacy, it was all a lie.

And his death really *was* just an accident. No, that wasn't entirely true. Evan wasn't the one driving. It was all Matt's fault. He killed his brother.

Sweat began forming on his brow as he leaned against the nearby wall of the water tank. Matt tried to control his breathing. He couldn't. Matt fell to the floor and began vomiting.

"Who the hell are you?"

It was a voice Matt didn't recognize. Who could be up here anyway? Matt looked up, wiping vomit from his mouth. He couldn't believe what he was seeing. There, standing mere feet in front of him, was Spark, the exact same costume, blond hair waving in the breeze.

"Evan?" Matt was in shock.

No, *you idiot*, he reminded himself. *Evan was never Spark*. Matt grabbed his head. He knew he wasn't thinking clearly.

"Who?" Spark asked. "Where'd you get my Spark suit? What the heck gave you the right to steal it!?! Do you have any idea how long it took to build another one?"

Matt was confused. "I-I-I didn't, I don't—" He began hyperventilating.

Spark looked at Matt with pity. Matt looked young, scared, and confused. "Listen, just—just calm down, alright. Just calm down, deep breaths. We'll talk this out." His voice was kind and soothing.

Matt took deep breaths, exhaling gradually. Head swimming, he stood up. He leaned against the wall, trying to steady himself.

"Are you okay, kid?" Spark sounded genuinely concerned.

Matt nodded. "Y-yeah, yeah, I'm just— I'll be okay." His voice was shaking. There was a lump in his throat. "I didn't steal anything. I only just figured this out myself."

Matt went on to explain about Evan's death, finding the suit and journals, everything. When he finished, he looked at Spark, who just stood unmoving as if contemplating his next move.

"I'm sorry about your brother," he said finally and sincerely.

Matt was startled by his understanding.

"He must've found out who I was, stole the suit, the journals..." His voice trailed off.

Matt felt uneasy. He didn't know how to respond.

"I need it back. The suit, the journals, the trunk, all of it."

Matt nodded. "Of course," he choked out. Although he knew none of this was his fault, he still felt ashamed.

"Meet me back here tomorrow, with everything. I don't need you running around in it anymore. I get it wasn't your fault, but that still doesn't make it okay." Spark's voice was commanding, like an authoritative parent. Like a hero should sound. Matt felt as though he let someone important down. "And wash the vomit off the suit," he added before flying off, without even looking back.

Matt slunk down to the floor, feeling lost, alone, and in shock. The air had suddenly become cold. The color had drained from his face. Matt's hands became numb. He looked at them, wondering if they were ever going to stop shaking. His days of being a superhero were over.

It's not like I wanted to be one in the first place anyway, he thought bitterly.

His only reason for doing it was a lie. The legacy, all of it, was based on a lie. Evan was a lie. A crazy fanboy stalker. A thief.

Matt's hair whipped in the breeze. He looked at the mask in his left hand as it rippled in the wind, and grasped it tight. The emotions swirled around inside him. Anger at himself for not figuring everything out sooner. The letter in the trunk was never even signed by Evan. He should have realized that it was written by someone else.

Matt gritted his teeth. He felt hate at Evan, simply for who he was. A liar and a thief. A feeling of hopelessness washed over him. Depression for losing the image he had of his brother. Loss of the suit. Of the ability to help people. Of flying. Matt felt a sense of betrayal, as Evan had hurt him more than any supervillain could. But most of all he felt guilt, for the love he still felt for Evan, and for ending his life. It wasn't a supervillain or a conspiracy, it was *his* stupid driving that killed his brother.

Looking back, he realized that he was so desperate to believe that it wasn't him, he held on to foolish theories, clinging to them when logically he shouldn't have. Matt sighed. He'd have to apologize to Dan. Again.

He closed his eyes. Matt still missed Evan, and he wished he didn't. He wished Evan was still here. And he wished Evan wasn't a lying thief. The cacophony of thoughts and sentiments raged through his mind. He wished he could just feel nothing. He wished he could just shut it all out.

I wish... I wish...

His head throbbed. He could wish for this and wish for that, but he knew it wouldn't change anything.

He didn't move for another hour. It had begun to drizzle by the time Matt finally, slowly, began lifting himself up. The suit suddenly felt like a burden, weighing him down. Every movement took effort.

Matt put on the mask and headed home.

CHAPTER FORTY-ONE

Class had started ten minutes ago. It was a Friday, and being the end of the week, the class was rowdier than usual. The class quieted down momentarily when a woman walked into the classroom, handing Mr. Winter a large box and handing him a memo.

Dan looked around. Matt wasn't here yet. He had called up last night sounding weird. He just apologized and hung up. Dan didn't even have an opportunity to respond, to let him know that he forgave him. He hated being in a fight with his best friend.

A few minutes later, Dan noticed Matt walk into class. Matt wasn't all that subtle about it either. He just walked in with no explanation, his eyes glazed over. Dan thought he looked like the walking dead.

Mr. Winter glanced at him, and seemed like he was about to question Matt as he stroked his mustache, before ultimately deciding not to, and continuing on with the class. Dan snuck out his phone under the desk, to text Matt, asking what was wrong. He pressed send.

Across the aisle, Matt's phone began making noise. Apparently, he hadn't bothered to set it on vibrate. The class and teacher looked at Matt as the phone continued to make noise. Matt seemed oblivious to it, his eyes still blank, his mind obviously elsewhere. A few kids sniggered. Mr. Winter's face reddened.

"Mr. Stone?"

Matt remained in his catatonic-like state. Someone tapped him on the shoulder. Matt suddenly blinked and looked up at Mr. Winter's reddened face. Matt quickly reached into his pocket and turned off his phone before silently handing it over.

"You can pick this up after class." Mr. Winter said, waving the phone, and placing it on top of the box. If Matt felt any emotion, his face didn't betray it. He remained silent until the end of the class.

By the time class had ended, most of the class was at the edge of their seats. They knew what was in the box. Mr. Winter called for an orderly line as everyone got to pick up their FalconTech tablets. Mr. Winter held up a tablet. It was a sleek, thin rectangle, with a sky-blue glossy finish, and a thick black rubber grip running along the left and right sides. The FalconTech logo appeared engraved prominently on the back in silver. It looked magnificent. Immediately, everyone excitedly rushed up to get their hands on one, except for Matt and Dan. Matt remained in his seat as Dan walked up to him.

Lines of worry crept along Dan's face. "Matt, what's wrong?"

Matt simply shrugged.

Well, at least I got a reaction, thought Dan. "Do you want to talk about it?"

Matt shrugged again.

It wasn't easy to just walk away, but Dan knew he wouldn't get anything more out of Matt. He was worried if he continued to prod him, he'd just explode, like he had before.

Dan nodded, walked to the front of the class, and calmly waited until he was handed a tablet and Matt's phone. He walked back to Matt and left the two items on his desk. Matt's expression remained unchanged. Dan took a tablet for himself on his way out. As he reached the door, he heard his name.

"Dan?" It was Matt. Dan looked at him. "Thanks," Matt said, his face looking as though he was in pain, like the mere act of talking required great effort.

Dan nodded and left the room.

At lunch, Dan sat next to Amy. Almost every other person there seemed to be glued to their new tablet, which Dan thought was fine, as that meant Steve was probably occupied. Plus people were slower to get to the food, and this being pizza day seemed to work in Dan's favor.

"So, you saw Matt today?" Amy inquired.

"If you mean the zombie formerly known as Matt, then yes," Dan replied.

"What happened? You spoke to him last! You didn't say something stupid, did you?"

"What? No! I spoke to him yesterday afternoon. We were talking about the tablets. He seemed pretty excited,

I think. I'm not sure. We also spoke about how there was some sort of a Spark sighting Wednesday night that Matt swore wasn't him. I guess it was a hoax or something Oh, and then we kinda got into a fight. He accused me of killing Evan, can you believe it?"

"He did what?!"

"It's fine. I think it was just momentary hysteria. He apologized later." Dan paused, thinking. "He's been acting weird ever since he got the footage of Spark being followed."

Amy looked thoughtful and began twirling her hair with her index finger. "Do you think he found out who it was?"

"Who orchestrated the hoax or who was following Spark?"

"I don't know. Either? Both?" She gasped. "Do you think they're connected?"

"That's unlikely." Dan sighed. "Look, you've known Matt longer than I have. He just shuts down like this sometimes. You know that. It's the kinda guy he is."

Amy looked unsure. "I'm going to try to talk to him after school. Maybe he'll be more receptive to me."

"Heh, I'll bet."

Amy shot him a confused look. "What does that mean?"

Dan shrugged and raised one eyebrow. Amy continued to look confused. He took the opportunity to change the subject.

"So, you know how to use the tablet?" he asked, tapping the tablet on Amy's side.

Amy smiled. "Not a clue," she giggled.

After school, Dan began walking to work. He was worried about Matt, but knew that Matt would tell him what was going on when he was ready. If Dan pushed him, he knew it could lead to another fight, something he wanted to avoid.

His phone started ringing. Dan looked at his phone. It was a number he didn't recognize. Odd. Other than Matt and Amy, no one ever really called him. He shrugged to himself and picked up the phone.

"Hello?"

"Hi there! How're you doing, Spark the Second?" Dan was surprised. He didn't recognize the voice. And who would be calling him Spark anyways?

"What?"

The man on the other side responded. "It's me, the Inventor! I supposed you're wondering how I got this number. Well, I scanned the phone while it was in your pocket on the roof the other night. Pretty clever, eh?"

Of course! Matt had Dan's phone on him that night. Dan knew he should've corrected the Inventor, tell him he has the wrong number, but he didn't.

"Go on," Dan said, in his best authoritative voice.

The Inventor began talking very fast. "Well, I've turned myself in, like I said. Currently awaiting trial. Anyway, the police began questioning me about my frequency emitter, you know, the one I used to unsuccessfully rob that bank a couple of months ago?"

"I didn't hear anything about you turning yourself in."

"Okay, fine, I lied. I'm a supervillain, what do you want from me? Anyway, the frequency emitter, it works by finding the frequency of something, like concrete or glass, and matching that frequency to shatter it, you know?"

"Mhm," Dan recalled having seen a documentary on Tesla a couple of years ago that discussed a similar concept.

The Inventor continued. "So apparently it's missing from police custody. Someone stole it from the evidence locker."

"What does that have to do with me?"

"Well, it can be very dangerous in the wrong hands, you understand. You should try to keep your eyes open is all I'm saying. You know, it's funny. The whole thing wasn't even my idea. Arthur Falcon was the one who tried to commission it."

Dan was surprised. "FalconTech Arthur Falcon?" he asked, unable to mask his shock. He couldn't believe his boss associated with criminals.

"Do you know any other?" The Inventor replied, laughing. "So anyway, I didn't trust him, a real unstable type, you know? So I decline. It was a solid idea though, based on Tesla's work, I'm sure you're familiar, and I couldn't turn down a challenge. So naturally, I made it for myself." He paused. "I should've realized Arthur'd see the news and know what it was. Dollars to donuts he has it. Yep, that's gotta be it. And he's gonna use it for Roddenberry knows what!" He paused again, as if thinking. "Eh, or he just might patent it and sell it to the military. Who knows?" he added.

"How do I know you're not lying again."

"You don't. In fact, there's a good chance I am. But if even one iota of what I'm saying is true—"

"Fine, I'll look into it," Dan replied.

He hung up the phone. Matt was useless now anyway, he reasoned. And Dan *knew* he could be a better hero than Matt ever was. He grinned.

This was his chance.

CHAPTER FORTY-TWO

Dan entered the FalconTech building, smiling and waving the security guard as he usually did. He couldn't believe he was actually going to do this. He knew if he was caught snooping around, it could mean losing his internship, or worse. Arthur Falcon was a powerful man. Dan began to sweat nervously.

Dan anxiously entered the elevator, awkwardly smiling at the woman already riding it. He pressed the button to take him to the thirteenth floor.

Most buildings don't have thirteenth floors, due to superstition. It was well known Arthur Falcon despised superstition and the like, and built the FalconTech building with his office on the thirteenth floor, just to spite the popular conception.

The elevator ride seemed to take longer than it should have. Dan looked at the floor to avoid eye contact with the other rider, fearful that his eyes would somehow give him away. Hearing the ding, he looked up. The yellow neon letters read 'thirteen.' As the doors opened, Dan found himself face to face with Arthur Falcon.

The man looked imposing at six-foot-five, with sharp, hawkish features. His blond hair was neatly gelled back and his green eyes looked intense. Unlike the heads of many tech companies, Arthur always wore a suit, and made it clear he looked down on those who didn't. He straightened his tie and nodded to the woman in the elevator as he walked in. Dan was ignored entirely. He quickly stepped out of the elevator and breathed a sigh of relief. He didn't realize he had been holding his breath the whole time.

Dan looked around as the elevator doors shut behind him. He had never been on this floor before. The thirteenth floor lobby was simple yet elegant. The floors were polished marble. Down the corridor was a mahogany wooden desk with a single receptionist. Near the desk, against the wall, there were four leather chairs. There were no paintings on the walls, and the only plant in sight was a single rose in a vase, resting on the receptionist's desk.

Dan approached the receptionist slowly, running through his plan over and over again in his mind. The receptionist noticed him coming and looked up from his paper. He was an aging man with grayed hair around his temples and glasses that rested on the edge of his nose. He wore a suit, despite it being casual Friday. Of course, working directly for someone like Falcon, that would be expected.

"Can I help you son?" the man asked. Dan looked down at his nametag. It read 'Larry Binder.'

"Well Larry, I—"

"Mr. Binder will do."

"Mr. Binder," Dan said, correcting himself, "I'm here to see Mr. Falcon."

Mr. Binder looked at his computer screen. "You don't have an appointment."

"Well yes, that's due to the sensitive nature of my visit. Mr. Falcon doesn't know about it yet."

The elderly man raised an eyebrow. "Doesn't know what?"

"I need to speak to him personally."

"Well he's not in at the moment, but you can take a seat here and wait."

"Of course," Dan said nodding. *Darn it! What do I do now?* "Um, excuse me, but do you have a restroom?"

The man nodded. "Yeah, right down there," he said as he motioned with his finger.

"Thanks!" Dan replied as he ran down the hall into the restroom. *This had better work*, he thought as he emptied a whole roll of toilet paper into the toilet. He flushed and raced outside to the old man, who squinted as his eyes scanned Dan, obviously annoyed.

"Excuse me, sir," Dan said urgently. "There seems to be something wrong in there. It's overflowing."

The man looked dumbfounded. "Are you kidding me!?"

The man stood up and cursed silently as he walked toward the bathroom. Dan had never been so nervous, and he couldn't believe it was actually working. As soon as Dan saw the door close, he ran behind the desk and pressed the buzzer, unlocking the door to Arthur Falcon's office.

As Dan entered the office, he closed the door behind him. The office was spacious. Two of the walls were windows overlooking the city. The view was gorgeous. The other two walls were unadorned, which Dan found odd for such an office. The room contained a comfortable looking leather couch, a few leather chairs, a beautiful, large desk with a swivel chair behind it, and a bookshelf with very few books. Dan sat down on the chair near the desk. The desk had a colander and a laptop on it, and a framed picture of Arthur Falcon with a former president. Dan wondered how he'd ever get access to the computer, but upon clicking the mouse, he discovered the computer was already logged in, no password required. Dan smiled. This was too easy.

After several minutes of searching the hard drive, Dan began to grow frustrated. There was nothing on any vibrational frequency device. Sweat began to form on his brow, which he quickly wiped away. He glanced at his phone. He'd been here too long. Arthur Falcon could be back any minute.

A realization suddenly dawned on him. Of course, he thought. Arthur Falcon would never leave incriminating evidence on a computer where it could be hacked. It'd have to be a hard copy.

Dan grabbed the desk's drawer on his right and pulled it open.

CHAPTER FORTY-THREE

Matt was walking home by himself, oblivious to everything around him. He wished he had never found the suit. He still couldn't believe Evan was a stalker and a thief.

Yeah, but you're a murderer, a little voice in his head said. What did that say about him? He killed his brother. *It wasn't really murder,* Matt told himself. *Probably manslaughter. As if that makes it better.*

The end result was the same. Evan was dead, and whatever kind of person he was, it was Matt's fault. If only Evan *was* Spark. If only someone else had been responsible for his death. But that wasn't the case. Evan was a stalker and a liar, and Matt was even worse.

Matt felt a build-up inside him of energy and emotion, but had no way to release it. He sighed. At least after today, it would all be behind him. He'd give up the suit and the journals, and maybe in a few months he could look back at it as just a bad dream. Maybe he could somehow put it all behind him.

"Matt!" His name suddenly rang out.

He turned, searching for the source of the voice. Amy ran up to him, before leaning on a nearby fence, out of breath. Her head was shiny with sweat, and mascara seemed somewhat smudged. Some of her hair was damp with perspiration and pasted to her head.

Holy smokes, Matt thought. *Even like this, she's beautiful.* He immediately felt guilty at the thought, though he wasn't sure why.

"I've been chasing you for like two blocks," she said, panting, trying to catch her breath. "What the heck, man? I called your name like five times."

"Sorry," Matt said with a shrug, blushing a little. "I didn't hear you."

"Yeah, I figured," Amy replied dryly. "What's up with you?" She looked at him, brows furrowed. "We're concerned. I'm concerned."

Matt looked away. How can he explain this? It's humiliating. He looked at her again. Those deep brown eyes stared back at him. Darn it. He didn't have a choice.

"Okay," he finally said, his breath shallow. "I'll tell you."

And he did. Everything just poured out. About the real Spark. About Evan being a stalker, stealing the suit. About his entire, albeit short, superhero career being based on a lie. About how ashamed he felt about it all. And how it turned out he was looking for answers and excuses where there weren't any. Evan's death lay solely on his shoulders. He had to stop several times in the course of talking, whenever he felt the tears welling up. He cried in front of her once already. He wouldn't do it again.

By the time he had finished, Matt was emotionally exhausted. Amy remained silent the entire time, and continued to be so after he had finished. Matt looked at her nervously, wondering what she was going to say, or if she'd even say anything at all. Part of him wanted compassion, but at the same time, part of him wanted her to yell at him. Call him any manner of horrific things. Because he deserved it.

"I understand," she finally said, slowly, as though every syllable was chosen with immense care. "I get it. But Matt, listen, yes, Evan was flawed. But being flawed doesn't mean he was a bad person. He was still the same person you knew. He was still your brother. And no, he wasn't perfect, but who of us are? He was human. Like all of us. It doesn't diminish his death or what he meant to you."

"But I—"

"I wasn't finished," Amy said, cutting him off. "What happened with Evan was an accident. You can't go through life blaming yourself. He wouldn't want that. And if things hadn't played out the way they did, you would never have used the suit. Who knows the effect you've had since you put it on. Just imagine if you hadn't stopped Blackout and he used his device near a hospital."

"Yeah, but—"

Amy cut him off again. "I'm just saying you need to accept what happened. Believe in a greater plan or whatever, or don't it doesn't matter. What happened, happened. You can't change that. Just move forward, and try to take the good out of it. That' all any of us can ever do."

Matt nodded slowly. He drew his mouth to a line as he tried not to tear up. Amy put her hand on Matt's shoulder, then drew him in for a hug. His heart jumped. He wasn't sure how he felt at the moment. A mixture of sadness, happiness, fear, self-pity, and guilt. One thing Matt was sure of though. He felt lucky to have such a good friend.

He held her tight, unwilling to let go for what felt like forever. As he finally began to pull away, he looked into her deep brown eyes. Those intense brown eyes. His view lowered. Those brilliant, small pink lips, slowly forming a stunning smile. He breathed in. Oh, the way her hair smelled.

She's gorgeous.

Without realizing it, he found himself closing his eyes, leaning in. Their lips met. Amy seemed surprised for a moment, before closing her eyes and melting into it. A jolt passed through Matt's body as his heart began to race. He could hear the blood coursing in his ears as he breathed her in. It felt unreal. He could hardly believe it, as he held Amy's face in his hands, with her arms around him. The moment was perfect.

Matt's phone began to ring. As she heard it, Amy's eyes opened and she pulled away. She looked at Matt, confused. Her cheeks turned red as she looked at him with wide eyes. Matt looked pretty confused himself.

"You should get that," she said, wiping her lips and looking away.

Matt nodded, his head feeling cloudy. "Yeah, yeah you're right." He picked up the phone.

"Hey, Matt? I'm surprised you picked up. It's Dan."

"Oh, hey Dan." Why did he suddenly feel guilty, like he was hiding something?

"Listen so I got a call from the Inventor—"

"What?" Matt interrupted.

"He thought I was you, long story," Dan said quickly. "So he said his vibrational frequency device was missing, and he thought Arthur Falcon might've taken it."

"Vibrational what?"

"What is he talking about?" Amy asked, still blushing. Matt turned the phone on speaker. He and Amy leaned in to listen.

Dan continued. "The vibrational frequency device. The Inventor used it to rob a bank some months back, remember?"

"Oh yeah, it can destroy metal?" Amy said.

"It can destroy *anything*," Dan corrected. "So I checked out Falcon's office, I'm there now, actually, and found some interesting documents. The device was built into the tablets. *All* of them. So the question—"

Dan was cut off. Matt heard a noise followed by a thud. "Dan!" he yelled. "Are you there?"

"What's going on?" Amy asked urgently. Matt held up a finger and pressed the phone harder to his ear.

A voice Matt didn't recognize came over the phone. It sounded strong. Confident. "I don't know who you are or what he told you, but you get yourself down here within the next fifteen minutes or this child gets a bullet in his head."

CHAPTER FORTY-FOUR

Matt's head was still swimming. This was too much. How could this even happen? He felt himself getting an anxiety attack. The past few days were far too overwhelming.

"Matt? We have to go over there!"

He snapped out of it. Amy was right. There was time to be overwhelmed later. Dan's life is on the line.

"Yeah, you're right," he said to Amy. "Run there now, I'll meet you there."

"Where are you going?" Amy asked, confused.

"I'm going to put on the suit." *One last time*, he silently told himself.

Amy nodded. "I'll call the cops. Remember, Falcon's office is on the thirteenth floor. Meet you there!" she said as she ran off.

Matt raced to his house.

Matt, clad in the Spark suit, landed in front of the FalconTech building. He looked around. He was sure he beat Amy there, but he wondered why the cops weren't here yet. Matt's phone buzzed. It was a text from Amy.

She said she was on her way, but apparently the police wouldn't take her seriously when she claimed Arthur Falcon, humanitarian and philanthropist, kidnapped and threatened to kill her friend. Matt sighed and walked inside the building. Looked like it was up to him.

As he walked down the corridor, he got a few stares. A lady started giggling. The security guard, a heavy man with a military haircut, wearing a scowl and dressed in a uniform that looked a size too small, began walking toward Spark. Matt shot him a look, causing him to pause. The guard then decided Spark wasn't worth the trouble and turned around, going back to his post. The elevator opened across the room, and Matt raced to it.

There was a woman in the elevator wearing glasses, three-inch heels, a tight skirt, and a white button-down shirt with the top few buttons not buttoned. She understandably seemed surprised to see Spark enter the elevator and press the button for the thirteenth floor. The woman smiled at him.

Unsure of how to react, Matt just nodded.

She winked at him, making Matt feel uneasy. How long does it take to go up a dozen floors anyway? The woman opened her mouth to speak, just as the ding sounded. Matt breathed a sigh of relief as the elevator doors opened.

Matt ran out the door and through the bare lobby, right passed the chairs, desk, and surprised elderly secretary, through the door.

He burst into Falcon's office and looked around. Dan was crumbled onto the floor in the corner. Matt ran to him, kneeling beside him. Dan's chest was slowly rising and falling. Thank goodness. He was still alive. Unconscious, but alive. Matt heard a faint click. Someone had closed the door.

"Well, I must say I'm surprised. I didn't expect *you* to show up," a powerful voice behind him said. "Surprising, the child knew a superhero."

Matt spun around. Arthur Falcon stood there, a smirk on his face. Matt stood up, eyes scanning the dangerous man in front of him.

"Well, I should've known *someone* would try to stop me," he chuckled, talking to himself. "As if anyone can." He began pacing the room, swinging the gun as he walked. "I don't understand why though. *I'm* the hero." Falcon looked at Spark, narrowing his eyes to slits, shaking the gun in his direction as he spoke. "How many people have you saved anyway? Ten, eleven, maybe?" Matt didn't answer. He knew in his few weeks on the job it was less than that anyway. "I'M SAVING A GENERATION!" Falcon yelled, spittle flying from his mouth.

"What's wrong with you?" Matt responded.

Arthur Falcon's eyes bulged. A vein began visibly throbbing on his forehead. "I'm a visionary! Do you even know what I'm doing? Do you know why?" He paused, expecting an answer to his questions. None came. He sighed in frustration and continued, "Allow me to give you a little lesson. All you kids need one. Besides, that's how these things work, right? You confront me, I tell you my plan?" Falcon smiled to himself, amused.

Matt stood there, unsure of how to react. He looked back at Dan. He had to get him out of there, but couldn't do it while Falcon had the gun.

"It's simple, really," Falcon explained. "Your generation is lost. America used to be great once, and New York was its crown jewel. New York even served as the capital of the United States for five years, until 1790. But now its youth is full of stupid, idiotic leeches, who will destroy our city, and ultimately our country. Now, not all of them, that's true. But enough of them to pose a threat. That's where I got the great idea to simply eliminate them."

Falcon smiled proudly as Matt's brow furrowed. *What was this guy getting at?*

Falcon continued, "So I put the vibrational frequency emitters in all the tablets, and gave them out to all of the underperforming schools in the city."

As it dawned on Matt, his eyes widened in horror.

"Now, the vibrational frequency emitter can be set to just about any frequency, and as a result, destroy it. That of rock, that of steel, or that of bone. Another interesting thing, young people's flesh, and yes, bones, vibrate at a different frequency than that of adults. I'm quite proud of it, really. And after I eliminate all of the undesirables, my city will be better off for it. I'm saving my city. *I'm* the hero here!"

"You can't be serious!" Matt exclaimed in shock.

"Oh, but I am," Falcon said, a sick grin plastered onto his face. He pulled a cell phone out of his pocket and began twirling it between his fingers. "You see, all I have to do is press the trigger app right here on this little phone, and all of the tablets will cleanse my city."

"You can't get away with this!" Matt cried. "I'll stop you!"

Arthur Falcon chuckled as he deliberately raised up the cell phone, showing it off the trigger icon. "Tell me, Spark, did you really think I'd tell you my plan if you have any chance of stopping me?"

Matt looked on, helpless, as Falcon caressed the phone.

Falcon smirked, and pressed the trigger.

CHAPTER FORTY-FIVE

The lights immediately turned off. The room was shadowed in darkness, with the only light coming in through the glass windows which made up two of the walls. It looked as if the power had been cut.

Arthur Falcon blinked, surprised. He looked at his phone. The screen had gone black. He continued to futilely press where the trigger icon had been on the blank screen seconds earlier.

"No, no, no, no, no! Why isn't this working?" He looked at Spark, hate burning in his eyes. "YOU!" he screamed.

Matt smiled and held up the electromagnetic pulse device, his finger on the button. The smile quickly faded as Falcon raised his gun. Matt dove as the gun went off. He could feel the bullet whiz by, mere inches from his face. Matt heard the glass shatter behind him. His heart was racing. He could feel the adrenaline pumping through his veins.

Matt charged at Falcon, who had begun shooting wildly. Matt felt a sharp sudden pain in his shoulder as he hit Falcon, knocking him to the ground. The gun flew from Falcon's hand and slid across the floor to the other side of the room.

Matt ended up on top of Falcon, who grabbed him and head-butted him in the jaw. Matt could taste the blood in his mouth. He rolled off Falcon, somehow getting out of his grip.

As he inhaled, the smell of gunpowder overpowered him. Suddenly, Matt was back in the car, Evan dying next to him. *My fault.* His head throbbed. *All my fault.* No, this couldn't be happening.

"I'm sorry!" Matt tried to scream, but it sounded like a whimper.

He could see Evan talking, but couldn't hear anything. The only sound Matt heard was the sound of his racing heart, thumping over and over. Loudly. Deafeningly. Then Evan slumped back. He lay there, motionless, his lifeless eyes open, staring at Matt hauntingly. *You did this to me,* they seemed to say. *How could you?*

Matt shook his head as he tried standing up. It wasn't real, he told himself. He had to focus on the present. Amy was right, looking back wouldn't do him any good. He felt weak. Just moving his arm hurt. Looking down, there was a trail of blood from his shoulder snaking down his arm to his hand. He pressed the button on his glove. Nothing. The suit wasn't working, he realized, and Falcon was much stronger than he was. Matt felt something grab his leg and suddenly tripped. He hit the floor. Hard.

Turning over, he saw Arthur Falcon towering over him. Matt experienced white blinding pain as the tip of Falcon's polished Italian shoe collided with his stomach.

Blood and spittle burst from his mouth across the floor. Matt groaned.

"You stupid kid!" Falcon yelled. "I'm a patriot!" He kicked Spark again, who turned over, moaning. "I'm trying to save this city."

Matt tried to lift himself up. Everything hurt. His vision blurred. He could just barely make out the gun, lying on the floor across the room. Matt slumped down. He couldn't get up. He didn't have the strength.

"You've only delayed me, you know," Falcon continued. "You haven't stopped me. Not even close."

Falcon looked down at Spark, who was soaked in his own little puddle of blood. Spark had begun crawling away. Falcon looked in the direction he was crawling, noticing the gun, lying on the floor near the shattered window.

"Ah, going after this, are we?" Falcon said as he calmly walked over to the gun and picked it up. "I'll ruin your name too," he gloated. "I'll tell the police that the demented Spark, possibly suffering from a psychotic break, walked into my building and killed my intern. I tried to stop him, but ultimately failed. At least I killed Spark in the process." He smiled, mockingly. "Then everyone will know I'm the hero. And a day or two later, I'll simply trigger the tablets, helping return my city to its former glory. Oh, this is going to be a wonderful week!"

Falcon began chuckling, then stopped as though he just remembered something important, drawing his mouth to a line as he raised the gun, aiming it at Spark's head.

I failed, Matt realized. I always fail.

He knew, in the back of his mind, this was always how it would end. In a body bag. There really wasn't a chance of growing old as a superhero. There was always, at some point down the line, a supervillain who would get lucky. A bullet would hit its mark, or just plain bad luck. But he didn't think it would happen this soon in his career. Or now, when he was just hours away from giving the hero life up.

What bothered him more was that he knew he would ruin the Spark name. He still associated it with Evan and found it hard to separate the two. This whole Spark endeavor was the only good thing that came out of that car accident. The only light in the darkness of Matt's mistake. And now it would mean nothing.

At *least I tried*, he thought, trying to comfort himself. He closed his eyes, prepared for the end.

There was a faint click.

The door, Falcon and Matt realized.

Matt's eyes shot open as he turned to look in the direction of the sound. What he saw was hard to make out at first, but it soon came into focus. It was Amy, standing near the desk, holding up a FalconTech tablet. She stood straight, trying to look confident, but her eyes betrayed how nervous and scared she really was.

Falcon looked confused. "Who the heck are you?" He then mumbled to himself "Why do I even *have* security? I really have to fire my secretary."

Amy's voice shook a little as she spoke. "I'm the person who just uploaded pictures of the documents on your desk online using this tablet. Within minutes everyone will know what you've planned."

"What?" Falcon said, as though he had trouble processing what was going on.

Amy tapped on the tablet. "And now I just uploaded a video of you saying you're going to trigger the thingy in the tablets. That's pretty incriminating, isn't it?" She smiled sweetly.

Arthur Falcon lowered his gun, looking lost. He began pacing the room, making wild motions with his hands. "No, no, no, I have to think, I have to think." Suddenly he stopped and looked at Amy confusingly, as though he was trying to piece a puzzle together. "But that doesn't make any sense. All the electronics are fried, so the Wi-Fi should be down too!"

Amy's eyes went wide, realized the bluff didn't work. Before Falcon could raise the gun, she threw the tablet at him and charged forward. The tablet hit Falcon in the face, and the gun went flying from his hands.

Falcon held his head, where it looked as though a bump was developing on his temple, over his left eye. His eyes bulged and spittle flew from his mouth as he yelled, "You little—"

He stopped and looked at Amy, who had his gun aiming at him. She was plainly nervous, as evidenced by the sweat on her face and her shaking hands. Falcon stared at her blankly as Amy cocked the gun. All strength and color drained from his face. He looked around, then back to her.

"There's no way out of this, is there?" he asked weakly.

Falcon turned and looked out the broken window. The whole wall was open to the city outside.

He muttered to himself, as though amused, "A little girl. Who would have thought?"

He turned back and looked down at Spark, who was struggling to get up. A faint smile grew across Falcon's lips.

"Well, at least I came close," he said.

He leaned backward and fell out the broken window.

As Arthur Falcon fell, the ground rushing up at him. He closed his eyes. Sleep came easily.

CHAPTER FORTY-SIX

Amy rushed over to Matt, kneeling next to him. Matt looked up at her, grateful and ashamed. She saved his life, possibly the life of tens of thousands of people. He shouldn't have needed her help.

Amy pulled off his mask. He knew he must've looked awful. There was already dried blood caked on his face. He swallowed, and could feel the blood as it slid down his throat. It tasted metallic.

Amy's eyes were wide with concern, as she saw his beat up face. She looked adorable. Matt looked away. Amy reached for his face. As she held his head, flakes of blood fell to the ground.

"Are you okay?" Amy asked softly. Her eyes began welling up with tears.

Matt coughed. Some blood dripped on the floor. "My shoulder?" he asked, his voice rough. It hurt just to talk.

Amy looked at it. It looked horrible. She wiped away the blood with her sleeve. "It just grazed you. There's no hole."

"Check on Dan," Matt said weakly.

Amy ran to Dan's side. There was a large bump on his forehead. "Dan? Dan, can you hear me?"

Dan's eye's slowly opened. "Amy? What're you doing here?" He sat up slowly, holding his head. "Geez, I got a headache."

He looked around at the blood-stained floor, Matt lying a few feet away, and the broken window.

"Holy smokes. What happened?" he asked, confused. "Is he okay?"

"I'm fine," Matt croaked, lifting himself from the floor, finally finding the strength to stand up. Everything ached. He leaned against the desk. "Amy, get Dan out of here. There were gunshots and a guy just jumped out a window. There's no way the police won't be here soon."

Amy nodded and began lifting Dan up. "What about you?" she asked.

"Wait, someone jumped out a window?" Dan exclaimed.

"I'll talk to the police," Matt replied. He lifted up the papers on the desk. "These are the plans for the tablets?"

Dan squinted. "Yeah, that's it."

"Great. I'll make sure the police see this," Matt said as he put on his mask.

He limped to the broken window. Below, he saw a couple of police cars had already arrived, and officers began roping off the portion of the sidewalk with Falcon's body. Matt turned toward Amy, who was helping Dan out the door. He nodded at her.

Matt was about to jump down, before remembering the suit was dead for the moment, and he probably had another five minutes until the suit powered up again. He limped to a chair, sat in it, and waited.

By the time the police arrived, the suit was powered up again. A thin brown-haired man began snapping pictures of the scene as others roped it off. A burly uniformed cop approached Matt and began asking questions. Matt calmly explained what had happened, what Falcon had planned, and handed over the papers.

The officer insisted they'd have to take Matt in for questioning, after a trip to the hospital. Matt nodded in response, stood up, and then ran right past him, jumping out the window.

While flying home, Matt had time to think. Just thinking about the past few weeks was draining. He still couldn't believe that he actually saved thousands of people. It seemed unreal. Then again, if it hadn't been for Amy, Matt knew he and Dan would be dead, and eventually Falcon would've succeeded. And if it hadn't been for Dan, Matt never would've been there to stop Falcon. It was a team effort, he realized, not his alone. But it was still a victory, and one Matt sorely needed after the past month.

He sighed. He was going to miss this. He finally got to be a real hero, finally got to save the day, and tonight he'd be handing back the suit, the journals, everything. There'd be no proof the past couple of months ever happened. But that isn't why he did all this, he reminded himself. He didn't become a hero for fame or anything like that.

It was for Evan. For his "legacy," which turned out to be a lie. But ultimately, something good *did* come out of it. Thousands of people are alive now because of the consequences of Evan's actions. And because of the accident. If Matt hadn't crashed the car, Evan would still be alive, but thousands of people would've died today. Matt still didn't know what to think of it all. Maybe life wasn't as random as he previously thought. Maybe there *was* some grand plan for everything.

Matt saw his house up ahead. He knew he would have to explain his injuries to his parents, at least the visible ones. After mulling it over, he decided he tripped and fell down the stairs. He'd say Dan was there and saw the whole thing.

Lying, that's what he'd be doing. How was that any different than what Evan had done? But Evan's lie had ultimately saved thousands, he remembered. Sometimes, doing the wrong things for the right reasons can be okay, can't it? But Evan didn't have good intentions, Matt reminded himself. At the very least, he probably had selfish ones.

As Matt landed on his roof and slipped into his window, he reminded himself of what Amy had said earlier. Yeah, Evan was flawed. But being flawed doesn't mean he was a bad person. He was still Matt's brother. And no, he wasn't perfect, but which one of us are? He was human. Like all of us. And that doesn't diminish his death or what he meant.

Matt smiled. In a way, Evan had saved them all.

The wind howled. Even in this cold, Matt had trouble keeping his eyes open. It had been a long, tiring day. Every muscle ached. Matt looked around the rooftop, despite the pain it caused in his neck. He was still the only one there.

Matt sat alone on the trunk, with the Spark suit and journals inside, waiting. He had called Dan after he'd gotten home, to make sure he was okay. He couldn't bring himself to call Amy. He didn't know what to say, so he thought it better to avoid it entirely.

The day's events played over and over again in Matt's head. He felt as though he should've been focusing on the fight. The events leading up to it. Everything that's happened to him the past couple of months. On *literally saving the city*. But he wasn't. No, Matt was thinking about something else entirely.

He'd kissed Amy.

It still felt unreal. Every time it played in his head, it was like watching someone else doing it. He wondered what that meant—if it changed anything. He did like her as a friend, he knew that, and she was freakin' adorable. He couldn't help but think that it might've been a mistake though. Why ruin a good thing? He liked his friendship with Amy, and he knew, just as most superheroes never made it past the two year mark, most high school relationships didn't last long either. He didn't want to lose his friendship with her, and if the relationship didn't work out, that would probably be inevitable. Matt shook his head, unsure.

But she's Amy.

Oddly, Matt found himself thinking of Anna, the blonde Russian college student from a couple of days ago. Man, she was *gorgeous*. Matt reasoned if he loved Amy in that way, if he was really in love with her, he shouldn't be able to think of another girl like that. But he did. And besides, he told himself, there are hotter girls out there than Amy.

Yeah, it's better for now if we just stay friends, he concluded. It was the smart thing to do. The only question now was how to tell her. It was a conversation he dreaded having.

"Hey, kid!"

Matt jumped, startled. Spark was standing in front of him. The real one. Matt was so deep in thought he didn't even notice him land.

"Hey, yeah, um, it's all in there." Matt gestured toward the trunk.

Spark nodded and walked up, opened the trunk, and looked inside. Matt felt insulted. He had shown up, hadn't he? Why didn't Spark trust him?

Something, it felt like a thick sheet, hit Matt in the head. Matt yanked it off, angrily.

"What the heck!?" He then noticed he was holding the Spark suit in his hands. He looked at it, confused. "I don't understand."

Spark closed the trunk and turned around to face Matt. "You think I don't watch the news? You saved more people today than I have throughout my entire career. I don't care how you got my suit, I'm just glad you did."

Matt was shocked. "I'm still lost," he said.

"The suit. It's yours." Spark sounded proud.

Matt tried to talk, but didn't know what to say. He looked up and said sincerely, "I won't let you down."

"I know," Spark responded. Matt could swear he could make out a smile beneath the mask.

"Wait," Matt said, as something just occurred to him. "Won't it get confusing? Two Sparks running around the city?"

"I got into a law school in Boston, so I'll be moving there before long," Spark said, matter-of-factly. "I'll still be back for summers though. Maybe we can team up some time."

Matt smiled wider than he thought possible. His cheeks hurt, but he didn't care. He didn't stop smiling his entire flight home.

CHAPTER FORTY-SEVEN

Matt slept through practically the whole weekend. He needed to, considering the beating his body went through. He wanted to tell Dan and Amy about getting to keep the suit, but preferred to do it in person. If he was being honest with himself, part waiting until Monday was so he wouldn't have to talk to Amy.

By the time Monday rolled around, Matt was feeling much better. Oh, sure, he was sore and banged up, but it was still a significant improvement.

He got to school early. Dan and Amy were already there. The swelling in Dan's head had gone down somewhat. Amy looked really cute. Matt began to have second thoughts about his decision. Dan and Amy were already in the middle of a conversation when Matt walked up to them.

Dan was talking excitedly. "I still don't understand how you expected it to work. All the Wi-Fi in the building was down because of the electromagnetic pulse. You must've known he'd realize that."

"I didn't know that," Amy said as a smile slowly formed. "Heck, I don't even know how to use the thing."

Dan burst out laughing.

"Hey, guys!"

"Oh, hey Matt!" Amy replied, suddenly looking somewhat uncomfortable. Matt avoided looking at her eyes.

Dan didn't seem aware of the tension between the two. "Oh, Matt, I actually looked into it. Turns out while the Inventor's vibrational frequency device *was* really stolen last week, the tablets were manufactured *way* before that."

Matt was puzzled. "And that means what?"

"The Inventor lied. He probably did sell Falcon the device, and then used us to clean up his mess."

"Oh," Matt replied. He wasn't sure how to react. He didn't like being manipulated, but at the same time, he realized the situation likely would've played out exactly the same if the Inventor had been honest with them.

"Hey, so you're ready to go back to boring civilian life, like the rest of us?" Dan asked, interrupting Matt's train of thought.

"You know that without you guys everyone here would be dead, including us," Matt said as he looked around the schoolyard. "I'd hardly call your civilian life boring. Or call you guys civilians, for that matter." He turned back to them. "We're a team. Team Spark," Matt said, his eyes meeting Amy's. They both blushed.

"We *were* a team, you mean," Amy said. "Spark's behind you now." She paused before correcting herself. "Behind *us*."

Matt grinned widely. "Not exactly."

Dan and Amy exchange inquisitive looks. "What?" they asked at the same time.

Matt looked both ways before leaning in. "Spark, the original one, I mean, told me to keep the suit. I *really* do have to learn how to fight though. I'll have to take karate classes or something."

"You're kidding!" Amy exclaimed.

"Oh man, that's awesome!" Dan said. "I've got all these great ideas to find higher..." His voice trailed off as his eyes looked past Matt.

Amy and Matt turned to see where Dan was looking. Matt rolled his eyes. Rose Ryan had just walked through the school gates.

"Are you serious? Dan, you're never going to—"

Dan interrupted Matt. "I almost died on Friday. That sorta puts things in perspective."

Amy nodded. "Like a postcard," she said slowly, as if just recalling something long forgotten.

Matt and Dan looked at her with puzzled expressions resting on their faces.

Amy explained. "I remember reading somewhere that life is like a postcard. See, most postcards start off with plenty of space and large text. But by the time you reach the bottom, the text becomes cramped and illegible. You try to fill every inch of space because you realize you've run out of room. And most people, myself included, just go through life like that. Why take risks, you know? There's plenty of space. It's only when we realize we're getting to the end that we scramble to fit everything in. Because life is shorter than you think."

Dan nodded. "Well, I'm not going to wait anymore. I'm going to make the most of the space I have now."

He puffed out his chest as he walked past the two, toward Rose.

"Oh my gosh, I think he's really going to do it," Amy said, watching him. Matt scoffed.

Dan's heart was pounding as he got close to her. Rose's silky hair waved in the wind. Her bright red lipstick stood out on her pale face. His palms began to feel clammy.

"Hey Rose," he said as he approached her.

She looked at him, her eyes questioning, but her face smiling. "Hey. It's Don, right?"

"Dan, actually," he quickly corrected her as his breath became shallow. His throat suddenly became dry, and he found himself speaking in a lower voice than he intended. "I-I was wondering if, I mean I know you already, um, I was wondering if you'd like to go out with me." Dan swallowed. It was hard with a dry throat. Rose opened her mouth, but Dan quickly said, "Just, Just let me finish. So, I mean, I know you already have a boyfriend, I'm not expecting a 'yes,' but I've had a crush on you for two years, and I just want, I need to hear an answer, even if it's no—especially if it's no—just so I can move on." By now his face was a nearly purlplish red. "Okay, I'm done."

A small smile speed across Rose's face. "You're freakin' adorable! Has anybody told you that?" She giggled. Her hand touched Dan's arm. His heart skipped a beat. "By the way, I don't have a boyfriend. Who told you that?"

"Um, Steve. Well, he didn't say it so much as imply it. You know, like referring to you as 'his girl,' sitting with you at lunch, stuff like that."

Rose laughed. "Steve? He's such a freak. The only reason I have anything to do with him is because he's my cousin."

"Your cousin?" Dan said in disbelief, before laughing. He stopped suddenly. "Oh, um, you never did answer my—"

He was interrupted by Rose kissing him on the cheek. "I'd love to go out with you. Meet me here after school, okay?"

Dan just nodded slowly in shock. Rose smiled and began walking to the building entrance.

"I'm never washing this cheek again," Dan said to no one in particular.

Matt and Amy had been watching the whole thing.

"Well, how about that?" Matt said in disbelief.

Amy smiled, watching them. Matt looked at her and breathed a sigh of relief. It looked like Amy forgot about what happened between them. *Now we don't have to have an uncomfortable conversation,* he thought gladly. Matt hoped it could all just be avoided, and everything could just go back to normal.

Amy turned to Matt suddenly, with a serious look on her face. "We have to talk about what happened, you know."

Matt cursed silently to himself as his heart sunk. He had dreaded having this talk. "Yeah, I suppose we should. Listen, Amy..."

She looked at him. Matt averted her gaze. This was harder than he thought.

"I think it was just, I was feeling lost and upset and useless, you know. And you were there, and I needed you, and it's not that it wasn't good or anything, and it's not that you aren't awesome. You totally are. It's just, I mean—"

Amy cut him off. "I understand."

Matt glanced up at her. Amy's lips were drawn to a line as she tried not to betray her emotions, but Matt thought he could see the hurt in her eyes. His brow furrowed.

"You're my oldest and best friend, you know."

She smiled, although it looked like it was difficult for her to do so. "I know."

They both looked away from each other for a moment, in silence.

"So friends it is then," she said, finally.

Matt looked back at her, but she had already turned her head away and began walking to class. Matt just watched her walk away, and wondered if he'd made a mistake. He did the right thing, so why did his heart hurt?

A hand grabbed Matt's shoulder. His body jerked in alarm. "Hey, guess who has a date with Rose Ryan?"

Matt turned to see Dan's face, standing beside him with a grin so bright it could light a room. Matt forced himself to smile too. He *was* happy for Dan. Really. He just wasn't in the best of moods.

"Yeah, I saw. Pretty awesome," he said as his eyes lingered on Amy, who was still walking toward the school entrance slowly, as though deep in thought.

She turned and looked back in his direction, a sorrowful look in her eyes. Tears beginning to form around the edges. Matt just stared. *Man, she's beautiful,* he thought. *She's downright gorgeous.*

What have I done?

"Amy! Wait!" He ran towards her, faster than he needed to, leaving a confused yet still elated Dan behind him.

"What?" she answered brusquely. She tried to harden her face to stop her emotions from showing, but Matt saw through it. Amy was never good at hiding her emotions.

"I don't care," Matt said. Amy raised an eyebrow. Matt's breath was shallow. His heart pounded in his ears. Why was it so hard to breathe? "I don't care if this can ruin our friendship. You're worth the risk." He smiled, which took more effort than he expected. "My postcard doesn't need any more blank space."

Amy's brows furrowed. She looked confused. "I don't understand. Is this a joke?"

239

"Amy Hunter, will you go out with me?" As soon as the words left his mouth, he felt as though a heavy weight had been lifted off his chest. He could breathe again. He looked at Amy intensely.

She looked away for a second, then looked back at him. "What took so long?" She said with a smile spread across her face as she punched him playfully in the shoulder.

Pain shot through Matt's arm. "Ow!" He'd been shot in the shoulder only a few days before, and it was still sore.

"Ohmigosh! I totally forgot!" Amy cried out, concern painted on her face.

Matt strained a smile. "Guess you'll just have to kiss it to make it feel better," he said laughing. Amy smiled and punched him again.

CHAPTER FORTY-EIGHT

Matt stood atop the Manhattan Bridge, hair whipping in the wind. The cold didn't bother him. Not tonight. It seemed to him as though nothing could. He felt invincible. For the first time, he felt as though the Spark suit he was wearing was finally his own. It didn't belong to an anonymous adventurer, and it didn't have the specter of Evan hanging over it. Now it felt like it was his. For the first time ever, Matt was Spark.

He gazed out at the island across the East River. The Manhattan skyline, draped in neon lights, never looked more majestic.

I've got to take Amy up here, Matt thought. She'd love it.

He felt a vibration in his pocket. He took out his phone, glanced at the name, and answered.

"Hey Dan, how'd the date go?"

"It didn't," Dan said, though he didn't sound the least bit distressed.

"But she's still going out with you, right?" Matt asked as another breeze shot against his face, making his hair dance over his eyes.

"Oh, yeah," Dan answered with a chuckle. "We were actually hanging out for a bit after school, but she got a phone call, family thing or whatever, and had to go."

"That sucks."

"Not really. We rescheduled for tomorrow night. I've waited who-knows-how-long to go out with her, I can handle another twenty hours or so."

Matt smiled, though he knew Dan couldn't see it. It was nice hearing Dan happy.

"And what about you and Amy?"

"Oh, we're a couple now, I guess. Our first official date has to wait a few days though."

"Hm. She's gotta watch Marty, eh?"

"Yep. She's busy afternoons, I'm busy nights—"

"Don't worry, you guys'll make it work!" Dan said laughing.

Matt laughed too. It wasn't that there was anything funny, it was just felt good to be happy. For the first time in months, everything seemed right.

"So, have you got anything for me?" Matt asked, getting down to business.

"Not anything significant yet, wait, hold on," Dan fell silent. Matt tapped his foot impatiently as he listened to static. "Okay, so there's some sort of disturbance on the Brooklyn Bridge walkway, apparently. Are you anywhere near there?"

Matt looked to his left, the Brooklyn Bridge in his sights. "Yeah, I'm near."

He squinted, in an attempt to get a better look. It seemed quiet from where he was standing. Suddenly, bright orange erupted, igniting a portion of the bridge in flames.

"Holy smokes!" He jumped off and flew toward it.

"What is it?" Dan asked urgently.

"It looks like someone's trying to burn the thing down!"

"Matt, it just came in over the police band, it's the Pyromaniac!"

"Who?"

"The guy who lit that building on fire you almost died in?"

As Matt neared the bridge, he could see a man with a red shirt and orange hair, a gun breathing fire in hand, laughing as he danced with the flames. Matt aimed at him as he flew down.

He was Spark. And this was his city.

SHORT STORIES

WALKING THE WIRE

The department store had closed several hours ago. The lights were all turned off. No one was there, save for a lone man, sporting black from head to toe. He walked down the aisles, heading toward the manager's office in the back. The sound of his footsteps echoed loudly through the empty temple of capitalism and consumerism.

Joseph Flask considered himself to be a good man, which was not that surprising. Most people like to think of themselves as better than they are-including criminals. Even as he removed the cash from the safe and crammed the thick wads into his bulging backpack, he felt justified in doing so. He deserved it, after all. A lifetime of training and preparing, all on behalf of the American people, only to be thrown to the curb. There was nothing he could take that he wasn't owed. He hastily stuffed in the last few hundred dollar bills, then zipped the pack closed. It was all insured anyway, he reasoned. Just another victimless crime. No one would be hurt...

The exit was a few feet away, but Joseph didn't head for it. Instead, he sprinted up the stairs, racing past countless floor levels. Most people would've tired by now. Not him. Years of training, of being forced to run nearly every waking hour, run until every last one of his muscles screamed in agony had built up his resistance. Not much tired Joseph anymore.

He jogged up the final set of stairs and opened the door at the end of the corridor. A rush of cool air greeted him as he stepped out onto the roof. He inhaled, taking it in. It wasn't nearly as satisfying as it would have been had he not been wearing a face mask, but it was refreshing nonetheless.

Something caught Joseph's eye. A man stood on the ledge of the building opposite him, staring.

Well, this was embarrassing.

Like Joseph, he was dressed all in black, and a dark mask obscured his face. But there was no mistaking that tuft of blond hair that poked out above the mask, or the electric blue streaks down the arms. If that wasn't enough, the bold blue "S" emblazoned on his chest confirmed it. Joseph smiled as he recognized his old adversary. Spark.

He must've tripped some sort of silent alarm. He sighed, looking down at his nondescript black shirt and pants. Now he'd have to face Spark without his signature red-and-yellow costume.

Spark kept staring at him, never moving. *What is he waiting for?* Flask wondered, before running full speed toward him. As he neared the edge of the building, he noticed that, underneath the mask, Spark actually looked surprised. Odd. But no matter.

Joseph leapt into the air, reveling in the sensation of weightlessness—of freedom—before gravity took hold. Even after they took away everything, his endorsement deals, his trophies, his Olympic medal, this feeling was one thing they could never take away from him.

He landed on a narrow flagpole sticking out of the brick wall of the building, walked effortlessly across it, and sprang off the pole, and came to his feet on the building opposite, not a dozen feet away from Spark.

"What, you don't recognize me?" Flask asked with a smile he knew Spark couldn't see. "It's probably the black suit", he continued, "I didn't think my usual outfit would work for a nighttime burglary."

Spark simply stared at him, not saying a word. An uneasy feeling swept over Flask. Did Spark really not recognize him?

At last, Spark spoke. "I'm confused."

Flask rolled his eyes. Leave it to the idiots to become the heroes.

"Yes, well I suppose that makes sense. How many people heard of daytime burglaries?" he asked jokingly. "It's me, the Acrobat!" *As if there's anyone else who could perform the feats you just witnessed,* he mentally added.

"The Acrobat?" Spark said questioningly, as if he really didn't know.

Was he drunk? High? They'd faced each other countless times! Flask silently fumed. The least a hero should do before going out patrolling is be at least semi-competent.

Then Spark muttered something he couldn't quite make out. There were only two possibilities: Either Spark was speaking to some nonexistent people, and had completely lost his mind, or he was talking to somebody on a hands-free device, which was something Spark had never done before.

Flask was leaning more toward the crazy option, but decided to give his longtime foe the benefit of the doubt.

Flask cocked his head to the side. "Are you talking to someone?"

In a shockingly horrifying response, Spark put his hand on his hips in a stupidly cliché heroic pose.

"Ah, yes, the Acrobat. Well, Acro, I hope you made friends with lions in the circus, because you're about to join them in a cage!"

Flask shuddered. Yes, Spark had definitely lost it.

To Spark, he responded, "Seriously? That was pretty forced."

"I'm new at this!" Spark said defensively.

"At heroic banter? That's apparent. And since when did you make jokes?" *Seriously, this was really out of character.* Everyone knew Spark was more of the strong and silent type. Maybe he was trying to remake his image?

Spark charged at Flask clumsily, who easily dodged it. *This is just sad,* Flask thought. *He's been drinking. That's got to be it.* He shrugged. Well, he might as well have some fun with it.

"C'mon, is that all you got?" Flask taunted. "Go for the 'juggler!'" He snickered at his own admittedly terrible circus pun and charged at Spark, who had begun to brace himself.

Out of the corner of his eye, Flask noticed his adversary press a button on his gloves, and Spark's hands started to crackle with electricity. He felt rather irritated. Spark would have to actually get his hands on him if that trick was going to prove effective.

Flask laughed to himself as the muscles in this legs strained, coiling and releasing, propelling him through the air, right over Spark's outstretched hands. Upon landing, he aimed a kick at Spark's back, causing him to stumble forward. The whole maneuver was done with such grace and ease, an onlooker would think he was watching a ballet. He smiled. This was *exhilarating*.

Spark was speaking again. "Hey! Hey, shouldn't your name be the Gymnast or something?"

A *legitimate question*, Flask thought. That was what he really was, after all. But the Acrobat sounded so much better...

He chuckled as he stood at other edge of the building, balancing on one foot. At this point, he was just showing off.

"Come on," Flask taunted. "Are we going to fight, or are you just going to *clown* around? I promise this isn't a 'trap-ese!'"

Flask cringed at his own jokes. They were *awful*. He really ought to think before he spoke. He could feel

Spark's eyes on him, analyzing him, studying his movements, his patterns. Trying to predict where he'd go next. But Spark was wasting his time.

"Your puns are the *real* crime!" Spark cried out.

Really? They were still doing this clichéd drivel?

Suddenly, Spark was flying toward him at breakneck speed, as though propelled by rockets in his boots. At a closer glance, Flask realized this was exactly the case. Adrenaline pumped through Flask's body. Time itself seemed to slow.

A smile spread across Flask's face. He spread his arms, slowly leaned backward, and fell off the building. Before plummeting to the hard pavement, Flask flipped over and grabbed a window sill that jutted outward.

CRACK!

Pain shot through his body. The movement had dislocated his shoulder. No matter. He'd worry about it later. Flask pulled himself up with his good arm, gasping from the effort. He made it without a moment to spare.

A second later, Spark flew past, searching for him. He made a few passes in the area, looking slightly confused, before finally flying away for the last time, allowing Flask to breathe a sigh of relief.

Grimacing, he reset his shoulder, wincing from the pain, then leapt from sill to sill, working his way to the fire escape on the far side of the building. Flask unzipped the backpack, and after checking to make sure all the money was still there, he slung the bag over his shoulder and tore off his mask, revealing closely cropped auburn hair, prominent cheekbones, and a slightly hooked nose. Stuffing the mask into the bulging pack, he climbed down. Within seconds, he was just another face in the crowd.

There was definitely something off about Spark, no doubt about it. But that wasn't something that Joseph Flask was going to waste his time worrying about. After all, Spark was merely a cog in a corrupt government system. His well-being was of no concern to him.

As he rode the subway home, Flask noticed all the wealthy passengers getting off, leaving only the poor and unfortunate, who were in their station in life due to accident of birth, or rules put into play to place them at a disadvantage. And Flask, along with his downtrodden comrades, stepped off the train and entered a rotting, ramshackle neighborhood. Just as the government had planned, he was sure.

Flask was quite aware of his reputation in the media. A common thief and criminal. They had a point. He actually did steal. But if those fools would only pay attention, they'd realize he only stole what was rightfully his, what was rightfully *owed* to him. Everything he took was always covered by insurance or the government, both corrupt structures that deserved to be taken advantage of. They weren't people, just organizations.

His crimes were victimless. If he were to be accused of anything, it was being a hero.

Lost in thought, he wandered down the eerily silent street toward his small, modest apartment. With the cash he'd gotten tonight, he'd be able to take it easy the next couple of months. Maybe he'd even go on vacation. Somewhere sunny. California, perhaps. He could use some color. He grinned as he pictured himself relaxing on the beach. So lost was he in his daydream, Flask barely registered the large man in front of him—until he bumped into him.

"Sorry 'bout that," Flask mumbled.

The man turned around glaring. At six-foot-six and built like a linebacker, he towered menacingly over Flask's slight figure. A long, jagged scar, was slashed across the left side of his face. It looked exactly like a lightning bolt, and seemed too perfect, as though it were made deliberately.

The man's mouth was twisted into a grotesque frown. He stared at Flask for a moment, as if deciding what to do with him. "You knocked into me," he said finally.

"How observant," Flask mumbled to himself. "Yes, I apologized," he said more audibly.

The man examined him from head to toe. Flask understood. He was judging whether or not Flask would be able to take him in a fight.

On any other day, Flask would have no problem. But Flask was tired. His battle with Spark, as strange as it had been, had taken more out of him than he'd thought. He knew he *could* take this guy on, but he'd rather not.

"So, I guess I'll be going now," Flask said quietly, trying to sidle past the man.

A hand grabbed his shoulder and he whirled around. "Not so fast."

Really? He didn't want to deal with this now.

The man pulled a small but nasty looking knife from his coat pocket. It was small. And yet, Flask knew it could cause plenty of damage. It wouldn't be too difficult to avoid. But *what had driven this man to do this?* He looked into the man's eyes. Something that looked like fear flashed through them. Flask pitied the wretch.

The man held the knife to Flask's throat. "Your money," he said harshly.

Flask nodded. "You probably need it more than I do," he said calmly, taking off his backpack. He opened it to show the man the stacks of paper inside. The man's eyes grew wide.

"Keep it," Flask said with a smile, as he held out the backpack in front of the man.

Without hesitation, the scarred man snatched the backpack with eager hands and ran. For a moment, Flask watched him go. Then he shrugged and sauntered lazily down the street.

So his vacation would have to wait. He could always burgle another place tomorrow night. For now, he was tired and his bed beckoned.

Suddenly, a bloodcurdling shriek of terror cut through the silence of the late hour. Flask whipped around. It had come from that direction.

Sprinting toward the scream's point of origin, Flask's heart began to pound. The all too familiar feeling of dread had already begun to wash over him. He silently prayed it wasn't what he thought.

But as he rounded the corner, his suspicions were confirmed. There was an old, white-haired woman lying on the ground. Her shoes were missing. She wore a faded polka dot dress. A dark red stain bloomed across the front and slowly spread. Her skin had been dark but was now turning paler and paler as the blood drained from her lifeless body.

And standing over the body was the scarred man. His gleaming knife dripped crimson droplets onto the ground.

No.

The man looked up, noticing Flask. He grabbed a patched and torn purse off the body and ran off into the night.

Anger and confusion welled up inside Flask. *He had all the money he could need. Why rob again? Why kill?!* Yes, Flask himself was a thief and a criminal. But he didn't have victims. He was not like the soulless monster who did this. Flask clenched his fists. He could have stopped this. He *should* have. As he gritted his teeth, another thought passed through his head. *He could make sure this doesn't happen again.*

With that in mind, he raced down the street, determined to apprehend the scarred man.

Three blocks, two aching legs, and one burning chest later, Flask had to admit that he'd lost him. The killer was gone. He cursed silently as he tried to catch his breath, and began heading back toward his apartment. As he trudged down the street, he noticed a great deal of noise emanating from Dante's, his favorite bar. Apparently, it was still open. He shrugged to himself and stumbled in. *Might as well have a drink*, he reasoned.

The bar was mostly empty. There were a few people quietly nursing their beers, and in the corner was an old couple loudly arguing about mistakes they had made in years past that had no bearing on the present. Half the light bulbs in the establishment probably should have been replaced years ago, and the fixtures were so filthy that even the few that were working left the room dimly lit at best. Music played softly, to the point that one could tell it was being played, but couldn't put his finger on just what song or genre it was. It was more background noise than anything.

Some would have classified the bar as a dive, but Flask, and presumably other patrons, thought it felt cozy and intimate. Now Flask sat on a stool near the bar and waited to be served.

"Rough night?" Dante asked from the other side of the bar.

Dante was an overweight man who rarely smiled, although he always looked happy. He was bald, and had been for a long time, save for a few tufts of hair behind his ears. He was also more perceptive than most people suspected. Flask often wondered why he had chosen to run a bar when he could've been a psychologist or detective or something. Maybe he never really had a choice at all.

"You don't know the half of it," Flask answered, watching Dante pour him his usual pint. "I was just mugged."

Dante's eyes narrowed, and his fist tightened around the mug in his beefy hand. "Do you have any money, then?"

Flask looked up at him with dead eyes. "Dante," he said, the irritation apparent in his voice, "You know I'm good for it."

The man grunted in response and put down the beer before Flask.

"So what happened?"

"He needed my money, so I gave it to him," Flask said. He took a sip and grimaced. The beer was awful, cheap swill. But people didn't go to Dante's for high-quality drinks. They went there to be not drinking at home.

Flask went on speaking. "But that didn't stop him from mugging someone else a few minutes later."

"Did you go to the cops?" Dante asked.

Flask raised an eyebrow as he continued drinking.

"Oh, right," Dante said shaking his head. "You've got a problem with authority."

"I've got a problem with the *government*," Flask corrected. "They never help people like us, and you know it."

Dante grunted again and nodded. Flask sipped his beer slowly, lost in thought. Why would the man murder a defenseless woman when he already had all the money he could want? Perhaps some people were already too corrupted by the fixed, government-sponsored class-based society they spent their whole life in. But that didn't give anyone the right to commit a crime that hurt other people just like them. The government created enough victims without other people, like the scarred man, adding more to the list.

Flask knew the man had only been able to do it because Flask didn't stop him. And he would probably do it again and again. The more the thoughts swirled in his mind, the angrier he got. Flask lifted his sleeve to his mouth and wiped the foam left by the subpar beer. If he wasn't part of the solution, he was part of the problem. And he wouldn't allow himself to be part of the problem.

"Hey, Dante?" Flask asked, looked up from his drink. Dante was cleaning a mug with an old cloth. He looked at Flask but said nothing. Flask took that as a sign to continue. "Do you know of anyone with a lightning-bolt shaped scar?"

"You mean like Harry Potter?" Dante asked, chortling at what he must have considered a clever joke.

Flask gripped the mug tightly, but did not allow his annoyance to show on his face. "No, I mean a real person. The scar is on the left side of his face. Goes from his ear to his chin."

Dante looked at him like a deer caught in headlights. The color drained from his face. "Who wants to know?" he choked out.

"I'm just curious is all," Flask answered calmly.

Dante eyed him suspiciously. "You didn't hear nothin' from me, but yeah, I know a guy fittin' that description. Warren 'The Wizard' Bullock is his name. He works as an enforcer for the mob, sometimes works the protection racket. It ain't a regular thing, from what I understand. They just hire him when the need arises. What he does the rest of the time I don't know and don't want to. What's he to you anyway?"

Flask ignored the question.

"Can you tell me where to find him?"

"Hey, you still owe me for that drink. I ain't lettin' you off yourself just like that," said Dante scowling.

Flask stared at him, eyes narrowing. Dante fidgeted uncomfortably. Finally, he relented.

"I'll tell you, but it's your funeral," Dante said reluctantly. "I hear he hangs out at Rizzo's. More than that, I don't know."

Flask nodded and put down his drink. "Thanks, Dante," he said as he stood up and began heading toward the door.

"Don't give me no thanks. I didn't tell you nothin', you hear?" Dante yelled back. But by the time he finished the sentence, Flask was already out the door.

As soon as Joseph Flask closed the door to his apartment, he raced to his closet. Oh, he was tired, but that didn't matter anymore. Purpose filled his veins once again. He hadn't felt such a rush in months. As he opened his closet door he reached for his familiar red and yellow spandex bodysuit. He smiled as he put it on.

It had been too long since the Acrobat made a public appearance. And while he was no hero, and what he was about to do might cost him supervillain points, he had to send a message. He admired himself in the mirror, the yellow 'A' boldly standing out on his chest. Then, with a self-congratulatory smile and wink, he was out the door.

There's a stereotype about New Yorkers, about how they never seem to notice the strange and crazy things going on around them. But that isn't true at all. They notice. They just pretend not to. After all, when someone knows people expect them to act a certain way, they do their best to meet those expectations. And the people of New York are no different.

As Flask raced across rooftops, clad in his gaudy yellow and red acrobatic bodysuit, an old man walking by noticed him out of the corner of his eye. Naturally, after noticing such an odd sight, he wanted to look up. And why wouldn't he? It was human instinct. But he, like everyone else in the city, had an image to maintain. He was a New Yorker, after all. So he kept his eyes in front of him and continued on his way, willfully oblivious to the goings-on overhead.

Unlike Manhattan, the Bronx still has telephone poles. Flask was only a few buildings away from Rizzo's when he noticed the telephone poles not far in the distance, with a parade of shoes hanging on the wires. There's a popular rumor in the Bronx that the shoes hanging from electrical wires are an indication of drug activity, like some sort of not-so-secret code informing interested parties that drugs can be bought at the location below. However, like most rumors, there isn't any truth to it whatsoever. In actuality, it's an old tradition spanning back decades. Muggers would remove the shoes of their victims and throw them up onto a wire near their homes, so that every time they look out their windows, they could see their trophies. Proof to themselves and to others of those they'd attacked.

Even from several buildings' distance, Flask couldn't miss the brown pair of women's orthopedic shoes dangling from the wires, keeping company with half a dozen other pairs. He clenched his fist. He knew he was close.

Flask looked across the street. Despite being so high up, he could still hear the obnoxiously loud music emanating from the sordid night club. Rizzo's was a seedy joint, and Flask would rather not go in there if he could help it. And it looked like this was his lucky day.

The scarred man stumbled out of the front door, clearly inebriated. It looked as though Warren had been celebrating. Flask's eyes were drawn to the backpack full of money, which Warren seemed to be clutching as if it contained the secret to life, the universe, and everything.

As Warren staggered down the block, Flask silently followed him on the rooftops overhead. Reaching an apartment building Flask assumed was Warren's place of residence, a bleary-eyed Warren fumbled with his keys for a moment before managing to get the door open. Practically tripping over himself, he made his way inside. Flask waited patiently. It wouldn't be long now.

Flask knew he would have to watch carefully now, waiting for a light to flash on which would indicate which window housed the entrance to Warren's apartment. After a minute or so, a light came on in one of the previously dark windows. Flask couldn't believe his luck. The shades weren't even drawn. He could clearly see Warren, as he took the old lady's purse out of the backpack and started rifling through it. The contents did not seem to excite him too much, however, as he quickly dropped the purse on the couch and went off somewhere in the house, probably to bed.

Flask smiled. This was his chance. All he'd have to do was grab the bag and knife and turn it over to the police. They'd dust it for prints, and that would be that. Flask wasn't a big fan of the police, but if anyone deserved to be taken advantage of by the corrupt system, it was Warren. And he might as well recover his backpack full of money while he was at it.

There was an electrical wire running from the building Flask was standing on to a telephone pole, and from there the wire ran to Warren's building across the street. When the average person thinks of an acrobat, their mind usually goes straight to aerobatics, the high flying spectacle of leaping through the air, from one swing to the next. But as any acrobat will confess, the true measure of being an acrobat is not aerobatics. That's the easy stuff. No, the real measure of a true acrobat's ability is *balance*. The high wire act. Being able to walk across a thin cord as though one is strolling down the street. It is no easy task, although it is a useful one.

Electrical wires, however, complicate things even further. There's a common misconception that touching an electrical wire means instant death, but that is not true at all. For the electricity to be able to harm someone, they must be touching something other than the wire. They must be grounded. As long as someone is careful to just touch the wire itself, not a pole, not the ground, not another wire, then they're perfectly safe. That's how birds sit on them without any harmful effects. It is the reason why, when the situation allows, electrical companies will fix wires via helicopter as opposed to a basket crane. However, for an expert at the high wire, like Flask, the wire carrying a live electrical current was no different than a plain piece of string.

Flask jumped onto the electrical wire and walked across. As long as he was careful to avoid other wires and leap over the telephone pole, he'd be fine. Within seconds, Flask had made it to the roof of Warren's building. He carefully climbed down the fire escape, doing his best not to make any noise. He didn't want to tip Warren off until it was too late.

As he reached Warren's window, he jimmied it and breathed a sigh of relief. It was loose. *Unlocked*, he thought. *Good.* Unlocking the window from the outside would've taken time he didn't have. As he lifted up the window and slipped into the room, he glanced around, taking it all in. The purse was still lying there on the couch next to his backpack. He grinned as he picked up his backpack and looked inside. Most of the money was still there.

Vacation, here I come.

He grabbed the purse and put it in the backpack carefully, as not to smudge the prints, and slipped the backpack on.

Now the only thing left to do was recover the knife. He scanned the room, hoping it would stick out among its surroundings.

Nothing.

Then it occurred to Flask that Warren would likely try to wash off the blood, in which case the knife would be in the kitchen or bathroom. He worried for a moment that if the blood was washed off, there wouldn't be anything to tie Warren to the murder. Then Flask remembered that, according to the police procedurals he'd seen on television, washing blood with plain water wasn't enough to get rid of it entirely. He wasn't sure about the accuracy, but at this point, he had to hope that was indeed the case.

Deciding to check the bathroom first, he tiptoed toward the hall. The wooden floorboards creaked. As Flask rounded the corner, he found the knife. It was clenched in a very angry-looking Warren's fist.

Warren charged at Flask, slashing the knife wildly. It appeared the large man's drunken stupor had worn off. Flask knew in this enclosed space there was no way he could best Warren in a fight, especially when he was without a weapon of any kind.

He ran in the opposite direction, toward the window. Flask dived out, hitting the floor of the fire escape with a deafening clang, which reverberated throughout the structure. He ran up the stairs to the next level, breathing heavily. He was tired, and his lungs felt as though they were about to burst. There was another clang as the fire escape began to shake.

Flask looked back and saw a furious Warren advancing up the stairs behind him. Each step caused the flimsy metal to vibrate wildly.

Flask raced up the next three flights, too scared to look back. By the time he reached the roof, his muscles burned horribly. His heart beat wildly and he found he could barely stand.

There was a loud metallic noise that sounded as though it was closer than ever. Flask looked behind him, just as Warren climbed onto the roof, brandishing his knife menacingly.

"Nowhere to go, circus-man," he said with a smirk.

It was moments like these that he lived for.

Pushing his body to the limit, he leaped onto the nearby electrical wire. He wished he could see Warren's stupefied face, but there just wasn't time, and he wasn't about to try to upset his balance with his body being in the state it was in. He breathed a sigh of relief as he slowly walked across the wire to safety.

Suddenly, the wire shook wildly. Flask struggled to keep his balance.

What the heck was that?

He dared himself to look back. Behind him was Warren, standing on the wire, slowly making his way toward his prey.

Alarms went off in Flask's head. This was impossible. But here it was, happening. Flask scrambled as fast as he could to the other side. Every joint in his body screamed out in pain, but he pushed himself on.

He knew any other option meant death. Flask leaped over the telephone pole and landed safely on the wire on the other side.

Halfway there.

He continued walking, his knees buckling under the pressure. His bodysuit was plastered to him, drenched in sweat. The building was only a few feet away now.

Almost there.

Suddenly, there was a thunderous ZAP! followed by an earsplitting scream that echoed throughout the concrete canyons of the city.

Flask leaped to the building, landing safely, where he collapsed to the floor. He looked behind him and saw no sign of Warren anywhere. Glancing down at the poorly maintained sidewalk below, he saw a charred, lifeless body with blood pooling around it, and seeping into the cracks in the pavement. Flask laughed.

Apparently, no one had told Warren you couldn't touch the telephone pole and the wire at the same time. Justice, as Flask saw it, was finally served. He reached into his backpack, retrieving the purse, and threw it in Warren's direction.

After giving himself a few minutes to recover, Flask decided it was time to return home. His night had been long enough. However, instead of taking the rooftops this time, he decided to take the streets.

As Joseph Flask climbed into bed, he thought about his encounter with Spark at the beginning of the night. Spark said he should have been called the Gymnast, and perhaps that was true. That was what he'd called himself for most of his life. But as he'd grown older, he'd learned that people shouldn't be put in boxes.

In his own mind, he wasn't simply the villain they made him out to be. He was an acrobat, forever walking the high wire.

A SPARKED INTEREST

The hallway was dark. Most of the lights were burnt out, and the few that weren't seemed unusually dim.

The boy raised his fist to the apartment door, but stopped short of knocking. It wasn't unlike him to hesitate, but it was unlike him to be in this situation. He looked at the door curiously, as if questioning its reality, and concurrently the reality he resided in. It was something he'd thought about, something he'd planned, but no matter how much planning and thought goes into something, it's always different once it's actually happening. It exists so much and for so long in the mind, that once confronted in life, it feels unreal. The boy couldn't believe he was here. That this was real. How many times had he pictured this moment in his head? How many years had he pined for just one date? And now it was actually happening. He took a deep breath to quiet the butterflies that had evidently nested in his stomach and knocked on the door.

There was no instant reply, which worried the boy. It normally didn't take much to worry him, and bearing in mind that there wasn't much more in life he considered more important than this moment, he could safely say he had never been more on edge.

The boy sniffed. What was that smell?

His eyes bulged as he realized what it was. He quickly grabbed a handful of mints from his pocket and shoved them in his mouth, swirling them around before swallowing. He tapped his foot impatiently as he waited for the socially appropriate time to pass for when he could knock again. The boy raised his fist to the door again, although the two never made contact.

"Coming. Hold on just a sec!" a voice said from the other side of the door. The boy's heart skipped a beat. "I'm just getting ready."

The boy looked at his hands nervously. They were wet with perspiration. He quickly wiped them on his jeans. It wasn't like him to wear jeans, but it wasn't like him to go out on a date with a girl like Rose Ryan either. His friend, Amy, had recommended he wear them, and having no other venue for information concerning the female mind, he heeded her words.

The door opened, and the boy's heart slammed against the wall of his chest. Over and over it beat, faster than it ever had before. He'd never experienced anything quite like it. His chest actually hurt.

Before him stood the most beautiful girl he had ever seen in real life. She had these fantastic cheekbones, and these amazing deep-set brown eyes, graced with just the perfect amount of makeup. Under her small button nose was a perfect pair of glistening pink lips stretched into a smile. Her silky dark hair cascaded down over her black leather jacket, which was open, revealing a tight red t-shirt.

Rose was very petite, and her form-fitting clothes didn't try to hide it. Dan tried not to stare.

"Hey, Dan. Sorry to keep you waiting," Rose said. Her eyes sparkled. There was just something about them. They seemed to convey a combination of mischievousness and innocence, with a hint of danger.

Dan couldn't help but grin from ear to ear. "Oh, no worries. I wasn't waiting long."

The two of them walked down the dimly lit hall toward the stairs leading to the ground floor. Panic grabbed Dan again. He had done nothing but think of this moment for years, and now that it was actually here, he didn't know what to say. His mind was utterly blank.

A *compliment*, he thought. Yes, that should work. "You look gorgeous," he said. As he said it, he felt his face turning red, and he turned away.

"How can you tell?" she asked laughing. "You're not even looking at me."

"Oh, I've looked at you enough to know," he said automatically as they descended the staircase, immediately regretting the words as they left his lips. *Stupid*, he thought. *You sound like a total creep!* "That-That was really weird sounding, I didn't mean to..." His voice trailed off. At the moment nothing would've pleased Dan more than the ground opening up and swallowing him whole.

Rose giggled. "You're adorable, you know that?"

Dan blushed.

"I'll let you in on a little secret," Rose said as the two of them walked outside, into the brisk night air.

She leaned in close to him, so her lips were just centimeters away from his ear. Dan could feel her breath tickling him as Rose's melodic voice traveled down his ear canal. "I made you wait on purpose."

"Wait, what?" Dan asked as he pulled his ear away from her mouth, confused.

Rose giggled again. "We all do it. No girl actually still needs time to get ready for a date. We're finished getting ready a good half hour before the guy's supposed to show up. We just like to build up the suspense. Makes 'em nervous."

Dan chuckled. "Well, it certainly worked on me."

She grabbed his arm. Dan stopped to look at her. She had her mouth drawn to a line and her eyes were intense. "If you tell anyone about this, I'll have to kill you."

Dan looked at her for a moment, trying to read her face, then burst out laughing. Rose broke out into a wide grin. Of course, he expected her to be hilarious. She was perfect, after all.

As the two of them walked down the poorly illuminated street, Rose grabbed Dan's hand. He was taken by surprise. Dan had never dated before, and wasn't sure what to expect. Amy had told him that hand-holding was reserved for the second date. Rose noted Dan's puzzled look.

"You okay?"

"Yeah, I'm good. Just a little tense." Rose raised an eyebrow. "It's my first date," Dan explained.

"Oh," Rose said, a shell-shocked look on her face.

"Mhm," Dan replied, sure that he should elaborate and come up with an appropriate excuse. He found himself unable to do so.

"Really?" Rose asked, as if expecting a different answer.

"Well I've never actually wanted to date anyone before," Dan answered, hoping it was a suitable explanation and didn't make him sound like some sort of loser. "Until I met you, that is," he added.

Even in the light of the dimly lit Brooklyn street, Dan could see Rose's cheeks turn red. "That's really sweet."

Dan smiled to himself. "So what about you? I bet you've had lots of dates." He silently cursed himself as soon as he said the words, hoping he didn't sound like he was implying she got around or something.

Rose giggled. "No, not really. I mean, I had this one serious boyfriend a few years back, but that's really it."

Dan's heart jumped. A serious boyfriend? Who was he? What did they do together? Would she be comparing everything, every conversation, every kiss, to this other guy? His mind raced with flashes of images he knew didn't want to see and questions he knew he didn't want the answers to.

"Oh, cool," he said simply. He knew to ask anything more on the subject would make him seem insecure.

"So where are we going?" Rose asked as they crossed the street.

"Oh, um, you've already eaten, right?" Rose nodded. "So I was thinking we could go for a coffee. It'll give us a chance to just sit and talk, get to know each other better."

Rose chuckled. "Yeah, I hate it when guys just take me to the movies on the first date. Not that I don't like a free movie, but it's like, hello, isn't the point of dating to get to know the other person? You can't do that in a dark room not talking."

Dan nodded. "Yeah, I know."

She continued. "Well, you *can* get to know the other person in a biblical sense, I guess. But that's not why we're dating, right?"

She grinned as she looked at Dan, her mischievous eyes gleaming in the dark, moonless night. Dan could feel his ears turning red. In all his time imagining how the date would go, he didn't expect her to make such risqué jokes. He gave a weak laugh as a chill went up his spine. It didn't feel right. He expected the evening to be more... innocent.

At this point, they'd left the residential area behind. Small shops littered the sidewalk, although most of them were shuttered. There were a few convenience stores opened, one of which had a group of kids hanging around outside.

As they passed, Dan smelled something that reeked like skunk. He grimaced. Behind them, a disheveled man who looked like he was in his mid-twenties, with his pants hanging closer to his knees than his waist, whistled as his eyes followed Rose, focusing on the small of her back.

Dan's stomach churned. *Disgusting.* He glanced at Rose to find her smirking.

"Doesn't that bother you?"

"It used to," she answered, running her hand through her hair. "But honestly, I've come to like the attention. It makes me feel hot."

Dan couldn't believe what he was hearing. She wasn't anything like he'd imagined.

"Oh, c'mon," she added. "Don't tell me that you've never stared at me."

Dan's face reddened, visible even in the poor outdoor lighting. "W-well I've never *whistled!*" he said, getting flustered.

Rose smiled and shrugged. "It's harmless. Just a bit of attention, that's all. I'd never actually talk to them or anything."

As they reached the coffee shop, Dan hurried to be a few steps ahead of his date. Reaching the door before Rose, he held it open for her.

"My lady," he said, half-joking as he bowed his head.

"My, what a gentleman!" Rose replied in an exaggerated southern accent, as she put a hand to her chest, and used the other to fan her face. "I do declare!"

A grin spread across Dan's lips. Yes, *this* is what he expected from her. This is how Rose Ryan is *supposed* to act.

The coffee shop looked pretty run down for such a major chain. Most of the tabled looked sticky, as though the sugar-filled drinks that inevitably laced it were never cleaned off, at least not recently. The place was empty, other than two employees, and someone who Dan assumed was one of the employee's boyfriend.

Dan took Roses order as she settled into a booth, and returned with their coffees a few moments later. Rose had ordered a half-sweet, non-fat, caramel macchiato. *Whatever the heck that is*, Dan thought. He had simply ordered a plain black coffee.

The truth was, Dan didn't even like coffee. He'd tried it a few times, but for whatever reason, he never liked the taste. He didn't want to come across as a child though, ordering hot cocoa or whatever, so coffee it was.

"So," Rose began. "Tell me something about yourself."

Dan thought for a moment, but his mind remained empty. There was too much to say, and thus nothing to say at all. "That's an awfully vague request," Dan said finally, as he held the coffee like a prop, pretending to take a sip.

"I mean like something very few people know about you. Something you wouldn't know at first glance."

Dan pondered the question, taking another fake sip of his coffee. "Well, I'm not entirely an only child. I mean, I am, but I wasn't always." Rose leaned in closer, her face displaying a puzzled look. Dan continued. "I'm a twinless twin. I had a twin sister, but she was a stillborn."

"Oh gosh, I'm so sorry."

Dan shrugged. "I never really knew her. I mean, she was gone before I was born. Don't think it did much for my parents' relationship though."

Rose looked at him with furrowed brows, as though she was worried about him. This was the last thing Dan wanted: to be a pity case.

"It's not as uncommon as you think," he added, hoping to remove the look from her face. "Elvis was a twinless twin too."

"Oh, cool," Rose said, worry and concern draining from her face.

Dan breathed a sigh of relief. "Your turn," he said. "Tell me something about yourself."

Rose bit her lower lip as she thought for a moment. "Okay," she finally said, looking around and then leaning in, close to Dan. "But I really shouldn't be telling you, so you have to keep it between us."

Dan nodded. "Of course," he said. It was exhilarating, being so close to her. An exciting jolt of electricity shot up his spine. Dan inhaled. He could smell her perfume as it made its way up his nostrils. She smelled like flowers.

"Well," Rose began, her eyes wild, with excitement emanated from her face. "I actually got left back a number of years ago. I lie to everyone about my age because I don't want to stick out in school."

"So you're actually eighteen?" Dan asked, surprised.

Rose nodded. "I didn't want to be known as the freak, so I don't let anyone know. Even on my social media pages, it doesn't have my real age."

"Why were you left back? I mean, if you don't want to tell you don't have to, I just—"

"I beat up someone in middle school. I don't want to talk about the details, but I sent him to the hospital. I was kicked out. It was a small town, so we had to move. By the time we found a new school that would take me, I'd missed too much. So I was left back a year."

"And the kid you beat up?"

Roses face hardened and her fist clenched. "The person I beat up *deserved* it," she said in a low, almost menacing voice. Every syllable was dripping with revulsion. "I don't know what happened to him—if he recovered or whatever—but honestly, if I could go back, I'd do it all over again."

She glared at Dan with an intensity he'd never seen before. He found his heart pounding against his chest, this time not from excitement or love, but from fear. Dread washed over him. *Who was this girl?* She wasn't at all like he had imagined. There was obviously more to that story, but Dan knew better than to ask.

"Excuse me," came an alien voice, cutting through the tension with all the care of a stampeding rhinoceros. Dan and Rose looked up. One of the coffee shop employees was standing over them, smiling sweetly. "We're closing now," she said, glancing back at her boyfriend and giving him a wink. "So if you don't mind leaving?"

She finished the sentence like it was a question, but Dan knew it wasn't. They were being kicked out. His mind raced. He didn't plan for this. He didn't have a backup plan. Dan cursed under his breath as he exited the booth, coffee in hand. Rose followed, a sour look on her face.

"I'm really sorry about that," Dan said to Rose as they headed to the door, hoping this incident didn't ruin the whole date.

"It's fine," Rose grumbled, although her facial expressions clearly conveyed it wasn't.

As soon as they exited the shop, Dan realized his glasses had fogged up.

"Can you hold this?" He asked, handing Rose his coffee.

Dan took off his glasses and rubbed them in his shirt before putting them back on. It was still fogged up. That's when Dan realized it wasn't the glasses. A dense fog had rolled in. It was like trying to see through a murky lake. *Well, this is just swell,* he thought sarcastically.

"Um, Dan?"

Dan snapped away from his own thoughts and turned toward Rose. "Yes?"

"Why is the cup still entirely full? Did you drink *any* of it?" She sniffed it. "And is that *plain* coffee?"

Dan blushed. How can he not look like a loser now? "Oh, um, I don't really drink coffee." He turned away from her. *This is humiliating.*

"So why'd you order it?"

"Well I didn't want you to think I was like, I kid or something, if I just ordered hot cocoa."

Her eyes narrowed. "How shallow do you think I am? As if I care that you don't drink coffee!"

"Look, I know—"

"What I *do* care about is someone not being honest about who they are. We might've well gone to the movies if you're going to spend this date hiding the real you."

Dan had never wanted to ground to swallow him up whole as much as he did at that moment. "Y-you're right," he said, his voice quivering. "I just got nervous—"

"It's fine," Rose said, before grabbing Dan's arm. "But you've got to be honest from now on."

Dan nodded. His whole body suddenly felt numb, as though electricity was rapidly coursing from Rose's fingertips through him.

Rose is touching my arm!

She let go, and the two began walking through the fog. To where, Dan didn't know, and at the moment he didn't care. He was still on a high from Rose's touch.

"I mean, have you ever even *tried* coffee?"

"Yeah, a few times. I didn't like it."

"What about flavored coffee?"

Dan stuttered, "W-well no, but I *know* I don't like it."

"You can't *know* if you've never tried it!" Rose insisted. A sly smile spread across her face. She held out her half-empty cup. "Try mine," she said. It wasn't a request.

Dan looked down at the cup in her hand and grimaced. There was no way out of this. He grabbed to cup from her and took a sip. He could taste the vile concoction as it traveled down his throat. His face twisted into a look of pure discomfort. He spit whatever little was still in his mouth onto the ground. "Oh, that was awful!"

Rose giggled and grabbed back the cup. "Now you're being honest." Dan smiled. "So where are we going now?" Rose asked.

Dan shrugged. "I don't know. I thought that coffee place was one of those 24-hour places."

"Well there's a park nearby, we can go there. Hang out on a bench or something."

"Yeah, sounds good," Dan replied as the two resumed walking. "So what's it like being eighteen? You're like, legal now and everything."

"It's a pointless age, really. I mean, at seventeen you can drive and go to R-rated movies, so what can I do? Vote? Whoohoo." Rose crossed her eyes and stuck out her tongue. Dan chuckled. "I guess I could legally buy cigarettes," she added. "But it's not like any place gave me a hard time before. They never give girls a hard time. Wait, isn't the new age to legally buy cigs twenty-one? Eh, so I guess there's no advantage to being eighteen whatsoever."

Dan was having trouble wrapping his brain around what he'd just heard. "You smoke?" he exclaimed. How could he not know that about her?

Rose shrugged. "It's no big deal. I don't do it all the time."

"But it's dangerous!" he said forcefully.

Her lips formed a sly grin. "*Life* is dangerous, my friend."

Rose looked at Dan. Her expression softened when she saw the shock and dread in his eyes. She sighed. "Look, I know it's not healthy. I know it kills people."

By this point, they'd reached the park. Rose sat down on the nearest bench. Dan sat beside her.

"I live with just my mom, you know," Rose said, although Dan didn't understand what that had to do with anything.

"Oh yeah? Me too. My dad moved out not long ago."

"Hm. Well, my father's dead," she said, as if the two were having some perverse contest about whose family life sucks more.

Dan wasn't sure how to react to that. "Oh, wow. I'm sorry. I didn't know." After a brief pause, he asked, "How did it happen? If you don't mind me asking."

Rose's face hardened. This was obviously difficult for her to talk about, and she was doing her best to put up a tough front. "Lung cancer. And before you ask, no, he wasn't a smoker. But that didn't matter, did it?" Her voice cracked. "So the way I figure it, who cares what you do? It doesn't matter. I'm probably going to die young anyway." She looked away from him as her eyes began to well up.

Dan wasn't sure how to react, so he just sat there like a statue, unmoving, his face betraying no emotion. He felt a cold breeze on his face, but it didn't move the surrounding fog. He could hear the trees rustling in the wind. After a period of silence, Dan finally spoke. "What about your mom?"

Rose wiped her face and looked at him, confused. "What about her?"

"Well, how would she feel if you followed your dad?"

Rose sat silently, unwilling to answer. She had her head turned away from Dan, refusing to make any sort of eye contact.

Great, Dan thought. Now I've upset her.

He sighed. "Where do you see yourself in ten years?" Dan asked.

Rose shrugged and turned back to him. "I don't know. I've never really given it much thought. I don't even know where I'm going to be *two* years from now, much less ten." She paused for a moment. "What about you?"

Dan didn't have to think long. This was something he'd actually given a lot of thought about. He looked up at the sky, although due to the fog he could barely make out the trees, much less the stars or moon.

"Working at a job, probably in the field of marketing," he said. "Maybe even in the process of opening my own firm. And a wife, maybe a kid. And a house in the suburbs. The American dream, I guess."

Rose chuckled. "A wife, two-point-five children, and a white picket fence? That's your dream? Don't you want to, I don't know, see the world or something?"

"Not really. Anything I need to know about the world I can learn from a book or documentary. I'm happy where I am. And I want to be in a position to provide a better life for my kids than I had. You can't do that when you spend all your money on traveling."

Rose looked at him with raised eyebrows, utterly bewildered. "But you need to *experience* the world. You can't get that from a book or a documentary. You need to *live* it."

"Tonight I had a half-sweet, non-fat, caramel macchiato. That's enough experiencing for now, thank you very much."

Rose giggled. "Oh is it?" Her perfect, glistening lips formed a mischievous smile. Her deep-set eyes narrowed as she slowly raised an eyebrow. "You sure you don't want to experience just a little more tonight?" she whispered as she leaned in close to him, her dark eyes locked on his.

Despite the cold, droplets of sweat began to form on Dan's brow. Rose got closer. He could feel her hot breath on his face. His heartbeat sped up rapidly. His mind raced. *What's going on? I'm not prepared for this!* He could feel his face turn red as Rose's lips neared his. Both were breathing heavily by now.

"I-I've never—"

Rose lunged at him. Her lips met his.

Dan was in shock. He could feel electricity coursing through his body. He inhaled. Her smell overwhelmed his senses. Time had suddenly slowed down. He'd never felt anything like this before. Her lips were slippery and soft, like clouds or marshmallows, her taste like something he couldn't describe, her scent like nothing he'd ever smelled.

Dan broke away and looked into her beautiful eyes. Her cheeks had turned blush. She stared back at him, her breathing labored, as she reached over and lifted up his glasses. Grabbing his head, she brought him toward her again, and the two locked lips for the second time. Dan put his arms around her as he breathed her in, her taste intoxicating. After what felt like the best five minutes of Dan's life, the two broke away.

Dan breathed heavily, as if he'd just ran a marathon. "That—that was amazing!" he exclaimed.

Rose gasped for breath, her chest heaving. She smiled at Dan. "You were saying?"

Dan smiled sheepishly. "Experience suits me just fine," he said with a laugh.

Rose grabbed his hand and held it, and leaned her head on his shoulder. Dan could hardly believe any of this had actually happened. He'd *actually* kissed a girl.

And not just any girl, but *Rose Ryan*.

And here she was, with her head on his shoulder. It was unreal. He reached over with his free hand and ran it through her silky black hair. They sat there for ten minutes—neither of them saying a word—until Rose broke the silence.

"When you said 'I've never—mmmhphmmph,'" she said, imitating the sound of their kiss, "Did you mean that you've never actually kissed?"

"Well like I said, I've never dated, so no, I never actually kissed."

"Not even like, spin the bottle or anything? Like, when you were younger?"

Dan shook his head as a wave a dread passed through him. His brow furrowed as he looked at Rose intensely. "Was I *that* bad?"

She chuckled. "No, you were good. I'm just trying to wrap my head around being your first kiss. How was it for you?"

"Well like I already said, it was amazing. Not that I have anything to compare it to."

"Hm. That's too bad," Rose said, raising her head and looking at him. "I mean, I'm a really good kisser. Now you'll compare all your future kisses with other people to me, so they'll all suck."

Dan smiled. "What makes you think I'll ever be kissing other people?" Suddenly a rush of adrenaline ran through him as he realized what he had just said. He began speaking rapidly, trying to desperately recover. "I mean, I know this is our first date and all. I wasn't being weird and implying that I'm sure you're the girl I'd be with for the rest of my life or anything, I just—"

"Shhh!" Rose whispered as she raised a finger to Dan's lips. "It was cute. Don't ruin it." She rested her head back on his shoulder.

They sat there for a little while in silence, just enjoying each other's company. All of a sudden, Dan heard something. There was a noise that had cut through the silence, faint and hard to make out. Dan jerked up, unintentionally knocking Rose away from his shoulder.

"What is it?" Rose said, alarmed.

Dan held up a finger to his lips as he strained his ears. Rose looked at him intently, a worried look on her face. Dan had heard something. He was sure of it. It sounded like two people in a heated argument. He scanned the park to see where it was coming from, but it was impossible to see anything through the thick coating of fog.

He turned toward Rose. "Is this a safe place?"

She chuckled. "I don't think *any* park is safe at eleven-thirty at night," Rose said with a smile.

"Eleven-thirty? Is it really that late?" Dan checked his phone. *Holy smokes.* "We should head back," he said. "I'd hate to have our bodies discovered by some jogger in the morning."

Rose giggled. The two got up and headed toward the park exit.

As they left the park, Rose reached into her jacket pocket and took out a pack of cigarettes. Dan watched her, surprised. Was she really going to smoke right here, in front of him? Her eyes lingered on it for a moment before she threw it into a nearby garbage can. She looked up at Dan, as if looking for his approval and smiled. A grin spread across Dan's lips, as he grabbed her hand and walked her home.

When they reached the door of her apartment, Rose turned to Dan. "So, how would you say your first date was?"

"Well, you're a really good dater." He said with a grin. "Now I'll compare all my future dates with other people to you, so they'll all suck."

Rose giggled. "Really though. I mean, you—do you want to—"

"It wasn't what I expected," he said, cutting her off. "*You* weren't what I expected."

"Oh," Rose said quietly as her eyes fell to the ground. "I understand."

"Yeah, well it was my own fault. I mean, I've been into you for so long, I built up an image in my head of who you are, what kind of person you are. I formed a version of you in my head that was flawless. Perfect. My dream girl." He paused and looked at her. She was avoiding his gaze. "I was an idiot. I fell in love with the *idea* of Rose Ryan, and I mistook that for the real thing."

She raised her eyes to meet his, fear and sadness on her face. He'd never seen her so vulnerable before. He thought he saw her lower lip quivered a little, though it could have been his imagination.

"But you're not at all what I imagined," Dan continued. "You're someone else entirely. But you're real. And you're pretty darn amazing too. I'd like to get to know you better. I mean, if you'd be ok with it. No pressure."

Rose smiled wider than Dan had ever seen. "Yeah, I think I'd be ok with it. Honestly, I'm not sure what I was expecting when I agreed to this date, but it wasn't this."

Dan grinned.

"So I'll see you in school tomorrow then?"

Quick as a snake, Rose planted her lips on his cheek. "It's a date," she whispered as she stepped inside and close the door behind her.

Dan stood at the door unmoving for the longest time. He'd been standing in that exact spot just a few hours earlier, but he felt like a different person now. His *world* felt different. As he slowly headed down the stairs, he played the evening's events over in his head. It almost seemed like a dream.

He smiled to himself as he walked out into the foggy night, thinking of dreams to come.

A NOTE FROM THE AUTHOR

Dear Reader,

Thanks for reading this book. I really hope you enjoyed it. A sequel may happen someday, but at the moment I'm busy working on *Blackcoats*, another series you might like (which happens to feature a very familiar inventive criminal genius). As an independent author, I don't have a large publisher behind me. As such, I have to rely on fans to get the word out about my books. If you want to support me and my work, there are some simple ways to do so:

-Please leave a review on Amazon or Goodreads. This really helps someone decide whether or not to give a new book a try. It just takes a few minutes, and is one of the most helpful things you can do.

-Recommend the book to your friends, either in real life or social media (be sure to include a link, if possible). Word of mouth is the way most people find out about indie books like these, and would be a huge help to me.

-Visit www.MichaelLachmanWrites.com and sign up for the mailing list, so you can stay informed about when new books are released and receive sneak peeks of future releases, as well as other updates.

-Buy six dozen copies and give them out to everyone you know. (I'm kidding. Mostly. You CAN ask your library to stock the book though.)

Doing any of these would be a huge help and would go a long way in helping to support my writing, allowing me to continue to provide you with books you love (or at the very least, moderately enjoy). Thank you so much for your support.

Best,
Michael Lachman

ACKNOWLEDGEMENTS

This book had a long history, and has gone through countless variations before it ended up as the book you're holding. Spark began his life as the sidekick of a character in a comic I drew nearly twenty years ago, and although the story, even from its inception, has been about legacy, due to its long history, numerous people have contributed to Spark's development, and should be properly thanked.

First, I would like to thank my wife, Zahava, for not only helping with the editing of the second draft of this book, but for contributing what I believe became the best part of the story: the twist. I had initially intended Evan to actually be the original Spark. In the initial outline, the big twist revealed that Evan's death *was* just an accident, not some villain's elaborate scheme. I thought it was pretty clever and unexpected (if solely due to the common trope being otherwise), but my wife insisted that this was not a good enough twist, and suggested her own. While I loved the idea, I decided that I since I had already begun writing, the reveal would have to wait for the sequel. A friend of mine, and fellow writer, Akash Kashyap, who told me, "Don't waste your time writing a prequel just to set up a book you really want to write." It was good advice, and it caused me to change a decent amount of the book, making sure the reveal happened in this book *and* felt organic. I'd also like to thank Yehuda

Broderick for his input on the first chapter, as well as Aharon Weinstein, who gave feedback for the 'A Sparked Interest' short story, and more importantly, gave FalconTech its name. Chayala Nachum deserves thanks as well, for the wonderful editing she did on the short story, 'Walking the Wire.' I genuinely believe she raised up a merely mediocre short story into a fantastic one.

I'd be a pretty horrible writer if I didn't thank Julie Hall, who edited 'A Spark Ignites,' coming in at the eleventh hour and saving me from missing my self-imposed release date. My good friend, Avi Greenberger, was also a huge help, catching a bunch of embarrassing grammatical and factual errors I'd missed. I don't know what I'd have done without him.

No matter how great a book is, if no one gives it a second glance, it will stay on the shelf forever. Chances are, if you're holding it in your hands, it was because of the incredible cover. Fabián Cobos has my undying gratitude, for taking my childish doodle and turning it into a masterpiece.

This has gone on long enough. I get it. No one wants to read pages upon pages of thank yous. But there's still one last group of people I have to thank. It took nearly a twenty year journey, from my first badly drawn comic book to this very novel, and they've been supportive of me every step of the way. So finally, I'd like to thank my parents, for supporting Spark through all of its iterations.

ALSO BY MICHAEL LACHMAN

When Adam arrives home to find his house swarming
with government agents, he quickly discovers that his
father was a secret government scientist specializing in
fringe science and the paranormal. An agent reveals that
Adam's father was caught performing illegal experiments,
including genetically modifying Adam's DNA. Now, with
his father missing and the genetic tampering beginning
to take effect, Adam's only chance to find a cure is to help
the agency track down his father. The mystery deepens
as agents go missing, and all the evidence points to a man
long dead. With the clock ticking and hints of a mole
within the agency, Adam must uncover the traitor, find
his father, and secure a cure—before it's too late.

ABOUT THE AUTHOR

Michael Lachman has always had a passion for creating, even as a child. In elementary school he often spent his time writing and drawing his own comics, making copies on the school copy machine, and selling them for a quarter each. Over the years he has dabbled in programming and web design, as well as both computer and hand drawn animation. After graduating from college, Michael went on to pursue a career in law. He currently lives in New York with his wife and children.

www.ingramcontent.com/pod-product-compliance
Lightning Source LLC
Chambersburg PA
CBHW031952120726
47898CB00002BA/375